The spectators were going wild!
Roaring their hearts out for Aaron Kornylo's
spectacular comeback performance.

It was a moment of victory that Aaron himself
had never expected to see after his injury.

It was Katie's victory also. And her tears
now were for the months of bitterness and agony,
hard training and sheer effort that she had
shared with Aaron, coaching him back to
believe in himself.

CROSSBAR

A beautifully inspiring story
you won't be ashamed to cry over.

D1178550

CROSSBAR

JOHN GAULT

Based on the Screenplay by
KEITH LECKIE

SEAL BOOKS
McClelland and Stewart-Bantam Limited
Toronto

CROSSBAR
A Seal Book / September 1979

All rights reserved.
Copyright © 1979 by John Gault and Keith Leckie.
Cover art copyright © 1979 by Bantam Books, Inc.
This book may not be reproduced in whole or in part, by
mimeograph or any other means, without permission.
For information address: McClelland and Stewart-Bantam, Ltd.

ISBN 0–7704–1569–5

Seal Books are published by McClelland and Stewart-Bantam
Limited. Its trademark, consisting of the words "Seal Books"
and the portrayal of a seal, is the property of McClelland and
Stewart-Bantam Limited, 25 Hollinger Road, Toronto, Ontario
M4B 3G2. This trademark has been duly registered in the Trade-
marks Office of Canada. The trademark, consisting of the word
"Bantam" and the portrayal of a bantam, is the property of and
is used with the consent of Bantam Books, Inc., 666 Fifth Ave-
nue, New York, New York 10019. This trademark has been duly
registered in the Trademarks Office of Canada and elsewhere.

COVER PRINTED IN THE UNITED STATES OF AMERICA
TEXT PRINTED IN CANADA

To Newton's First Law

1

The sun had not risen high enough to warm the prairie day. By mid-afternoon it would be almost unbearable, but now it hung, reddish and lifeless, just over the top of the still-dewy wheat that stretched unbroken toward the eastern horizon. It was cold, cold enough for woolen sweaters and flannel shirts and for blowing on your hands when they start to stiffen. Still, Aaron Kornylo was sweating. He was also breathing heavily—actually gasping sometimes—and moaning and thrashing around in his bed, the quilt and blanket and sheet long-since kicked aside. His eyelids flickered wildly, threatening to open, *wanting* to open, to deliver him from this grotesque dream one more time. But no, first the noise—the machine's noise—would have to come, closer and closer and closer and . . . then the pain, so terrible that the brain, in its mysterious wisdom, shut down the system . . . just after the scream.

Aaron was suddenly upright, then leaning forward, gagging on the bile that was in his throat. Tears commingled with the sweat on his face, and his pale body shuddered under the clammy pajamas. Still in that passageway between sleep and consciousness, he swung his body into a sitting position and hurled himself toward the window, clamping his hands down on the sill. Out in the yard the great harvester sat there, the great drill-like auger at rest on a wooden block. No, he hadn't really heard it, that morning or any of the

1

other mornings since he'd been home from the hospital. In a few days, the weather willing, it would again lumber across the fields, scissoring off the wheat, filling the bins with golden kernels. But for the moment it just sat there, neither evil nor benign, unaware of, and unresponsible for, the terrible thing it had done to him.

Aaron, reassured, blinked himself awake. To fill the few seconds it required, he focused on the one movement that disturbed the peace of the prairie dawn: a solitary hawk spiraling earthward for its first gopher of the day. Aaron did not stay around for the inevitable conclusion—he'd seen it too many times before—and by now he was fully conscious anyway, beginning to feel the cold. He started quickly away from the window. Then, remembering, he reached for the crutches.

He was still awkward in the shower, despite the chrome grab-bars his father had installed a few days after his homecoming. Even something as normal and inevitable as dropping the soap required an irritating and clumsy ritual of recovery. He was handling the shaving and toothbrushing and hair-combing pretty well now, though: he could lean on his crutches for these things. Aaron opened the bathroom door a crack; no, neither of his parents was in the hall. Naked, his pajamas slung over his shoulder, he pushed off back to his room, droplets of water still glistening on his back.

The sunlight had slid down the wall and brought to life the glass and metal and polished wood that hung and stood there. The shadowy blacks and whites and greys took on their genuine colors: red and blue ribbons from almost-forgotten high school track meets, yellowed photos of a skinny blond boy in blue shorts, courtesy of the local newspapers, and faded stories about the exploits of the best athlete Willow Creek, Saskatchewan, had ever produced. Then, closer to the imaginary centre of the wall, a ring of more recent triumphs, medals of gold and silver from the Commonwealth Games, and the Pan-American Games, and from every major Canadian meet of the past five years. More photos, as likely to be from magazine color spreads now as from newspapers and wire services. Aaron rising majestically, haloed by the sun, his back arching over the crossbar; Aaron standing proud on the raised dais, between and above the men who finished second and third; Aaron being vested with his Commonwealth Games gold medal by Prince Charles himself, with an exchange of smiles. He often wished he'd remembered what the Prince had said to him that day; it would have been something to tell his grandchildren when they asked him for the twentieth time what the king and he had talked about, but he could not. He assumed that he, Aaron, had said something positively silly.

With what had once been smiling pride, but what had now become something closer to morbid fascination, Aaron Kornylo reviewed his life as it was represented by that wall. He read it from the periphery inward, to the small oak-and-glass case that the rosy sunlight was now bringing to life. The medal inside shone like the gold around it. But it was better. Much better.

It was only bronze, but it was the Olympic bronze. Three years ago Aaron Kornylo, the best high jumper in Canada (and, for that matter, the British Commonwealth) had become the third-best high jumper in the whole world. He closed his eyes and lowered his head and stood there naked in the door-frame and remembered Montreal.

A roaring choir of fifty thousand voices as his name is announced. Silence as he comes to his starting position. Fifty thousand chests expanded with pent-in breath. The second of fear and doubt. Then, self-induced peace. Now! Running. Now! Lift-off. Rising. Soaring. Twisting in the air. Tuck. Over now, free falling. And then explosions of sound. Lying in the mattresses. Arms up. People racing toward him. Shouts. Laughter.

Tears. Aaron wiped at his eyes, opened them, and returned to his room, to everything he had been and would never be again.

He didn't look that different, at least as far as the dresser mirror showed, which was from the thighs on up. The exercise program they'd forced him into at the hospital had kept the arms and back and upper torso in good tone and the gut, under the light blond hair, was flat and hard. His face, though. His face had changed: there was no longer any laughter there, no evidence to show that until a couple of months before Aaron Kornylo had enjoyed his personal version of the best of all possible worlds. The blue eyes were icy now, and what he'd once fancied was a sensual mouth had become just a functional slit, hiding teeth that seemed to be perpetually clenched. He tried to smile, but it didn't work: all he got was a clown face that wasn't happy and wasn't funny. A grimace.

The medal was drawing him again, making him look. It was hard, living in this room now, with the past mocking the present. Everybody said it would pass, that he'd get over it, that he'd adjust and be fine. He stared at the medal until the sunlight had passed it by and its sparkle was lost, until it sat there as cold and dead as it truly was.

"Like me," Aaron muttered. Only then did he look down at the rounded stump that had once been his right leg. The surgeons in Saskatoon had done a fine job, very neat. He could see that. Funny, but he didn't feel like giving thanks. And they'd told him he'd get used to it, and to the prosthesis they'd taught him to wear, that hated "wooden leg" that stood propped against the side of the dresser, right where he'd put it when he came home, and where, as far as he was concerned, it would stay. To hell with them, to hell with it and to hell with everything; if he was going to be a cripple, he was going to be a visible cripple. And all that meaningless crap about how he was lucky to be alive? Well, that's all it was—meaningless crap. Maybe there was more to life than jumping high in the air, but that remained to be seen.

He dropped back onto the bed, came up to a sitting position and rummaged the top drawer of his dresser for socks and underwear. The socks, yellow Adidas with two blue stripes at the top, were expertly rolled together. A slight smile flickered over his face as he considered his mother's handiwork. Then, with a shake of the head, he wiped the smile away, separated the socks and flung one of them back into the drawer.

"Okay, Aaron," he sighed. "Time to face another day."

Myles Kornylo was not a patient man. After a lifetime of farming, waiting for the snow to go and the sun and rain to come, he should have been. But he wasn't. He always seemed to be fighting things, like the damned broken trailer hitch he was attempting to repair at that very moment. Life had been an ongoing struggle for Myles Kornylo, much of it real and much of it created and exacerbated by the man himself. Taking over an 800-acre farm at seventeen had not been his idea. No, the only idea in his head at that time was that he might make it in pro hockey; people who *knew* were comparing him to that other small-town Saskatchewan boy, Gordie Howe, a few years older and already a star in Detroit. In fact, he looked like Howe, then and even now, all sinew and sloping shoulders and heavy forearms and lopsided grins.

But one day his father had come to him with a sad face and they'd walked out into the muddy spring fields and hockey and even high school were over. The doctors said his father's heart was going, and he had to take it easy. The farm belonged to Myles now. Either that or sell it.

Nearly thirty years later Myles Kornylo still wondered if he could have made it in the NHL, or if he could have made it through the University of Minnesota on that scholarship that was also being talked about for him. But he didn't think about it much, and he didn't talk about it at all.

He was, after all, a lucky man. He had the land, and it provided. He had his wife, Clare, who was far too pretty and far too smart to have stuck twenty-five years with anybody who really wasn't worth something. And he had his own son, Aaron: a good son, a gifted son, a son to make a father proud. But Myles never said these things, not because he didn't want to but because he didn't know how. He hoped that they'd all understand—his wife, his son, the land itself.

Through the smoked-glass window of the welder's mask he saw the jerry-rigged clamp fall away and the metal strut follow it. It was a two-man operation, and he'd known that from the start of it, but Myles was damned if he would ask anybody for help; if they couldn't see that he needed it, well to hell with them. He cursed, twisted off the oxyacetylene torch, and tossed it aside. He scraped his chin as he yanked off the mask, and stifled a second curse only because he sensed, by then, that he was being watched.

"Everything all right?" asked the woman who was watching. Clare dropped her clothespins into the big laundry hamper and ducked under the clothesline she'd been hanging the morning wash on. Just as Myles had wanted to swear, Clare had wanted to laugh. She always wanted to laugh when she saw her beloved husband doing these bullheaded things because they were . . . well . . . *endearing* in their own way. Myles was a luckier man than even he knew, because in Clare Collins Kornylo he had a wife who didn't need to be told how much she was loved and wanted, or when he was hurt and sad and depressed. Clare was one of those rare people who draw maximum emotional sustenance from a minimum of emotional massage. Even if he'd tried, Myles could not have hidden his love from her.

"Want some help with that?" she asked, surveying the damage.

"Where's Aaron?" he growled back, embarrassed that she'd seen his little performance.

"I can help as well as he can, you know."

"Don't need any help," Myles lied. "Just wondered where he was, that's all." What Myles really, truly wanted was just to have Aaron around him, like in the old days, to talk and share. He'd have liked the help too, if only because it was Aaron's. Mostly, though, it was the other things. And he needed to tell Aaron something: that he was sorry, that he hadn't seen him from the cab of the harvester until it was too late . . .

Clare returned to her clothesline.

"You think he's all right?" Myles asked. He had tried to make it a casual question, but it hadn't come out that way. He didn't know if his son was all right, but he suspected that Clare did. Clare knew these things, somehow, and she always seemed to know them without asking. Clare turned and met his searching gaze, held it for a few seconds, and nodded.

"He's got a lot of things to deal with," she said. "He's dealing with them as best he can. Like this morning: he actually went over to town to see about that job that was in the paper."

Myles' face hardened. Aaron had a job. Right here. The farm didn't run itself, and it didn't pay enough to provide for permanent hired help. Besides, now—especially now—the farm was Aaron's future, his one chance, more now than ever before.

"Waste of time," Myles said, turning his attention once again to the broken trailer hitch on the plough.

"His experience counts for something," Clare replied, her voice and its tone rising to his challenge. "It's what he knows how to do."

"He knows how to farm, to run a farm. His experience counts right here." Enough said, as far as he was concerned. There was a trailer hitch to repair and the sun was getting high. Ignoring Clare, he scanned the farmyard until he saw what he wanted, the chopping block which was just about the right height to suit his purposes. Clare waited patiently while he retrieved it, positioned it just right so it would take most of the weight of the metal strut. He slowly lined up the strut and replaced the clamp which, with the minimal weight it now had to accommodate, held just fine.

When his movements became less jerky (meaning he was calming down from his anger) Clare resumed the conversation.

"Myles, he may not want the farm. You know that and I know that. Is that what you're afraid of, that he won't? Is that why you're angry?"

"Not angry . . . Clare, the farm is all I have to give him."

For a very long moment they just stared at one another. Then Clare crossed the gulf and tucked herself into his arms and squeezed the hard flesh of his back. Hesitantly Myles responded, wrapping his big arms around the little woman whose head didn't even come up to his chin.

"No it isn't, Myles," she murmured into the pleasant-sweaty smell of his shirt. "You have much more to give him than that."

"But he's got to accept what he is, Clare."

"He does, Myles, he does. And he will. Right now he's got more than his share of accepting to do, hasn't he? Be patient, Myles. Please."

Myles left it at that. After a few moments they gently drew apart and he strode off toward the house without saying why. Clare watched, remembering how Aaron, even when he was a little boy, had fallen so naturally into that same walk—elbows out, legs slightly bowed, the head that never bobbed. Like father, like son as they say. In more ways than one, she added, not for the first time or even the tenth. Clare smiled and wiped a tear away and went back to her washing.

Everybody who knew the two of them seemed moved to comment on how much Katie Barlow resembled Katie Potts, who was her mother's favorite aunt and a raving beauty in her day. While Katie the younger did her damnedest not to acknowledge the comparison, she would, when nobody else was around, sit with the family album and stack herself up against Miss Winnipeg of 1927. There was, she had to admit, a resemblance—the dark, Cree eyes that appeared in the family about once a generation, the thick black hair that defied curl, and the nose just a touch too small for the strong face. But Katie Barlow was bigger and stronger than her aunt had ever been, which was either a result of being her father's daughter or all that extra nutrition she was supposed to have received.

And if there was a physical likeness, that's where it ended. Katie Potts had kept—along with her virtue—

the notion that young ladies did not perspire in public. Whenever she visited Willow Creek, or whenever she had her niece with her in Winnipeg, she did her best to push that philosophy home. Once she sent her namesake a copy of *Fascinating Womanhood*. Katie, in return, gave her aunt a copy of *The Female Eunuch*.

Katie Barlow was thinking about Katie Potts at that moment because the speedometer needle on the old white Chevy was crossing the eighty m.p.h. mark. If Katie Potts had known what Katie Barlow was doing to her beloved Chev at that moment (and at so many other moments) she'd have taken it back. Under her tender loving care it had never looked or sounded any different than the day she took it off the lot in 1963. Its oil was changed every thousand miles, it was washed every week, tuned up every spring and put up on blocks each winter. For the speedometer needle, anything above fifty m.p.h. had been virgin territory.

Katie the younger had promised to carry on the tradition, but it just wasn't in her. Oh, when her younger sister or her mother or some other adult was in the car, and when she was driving in town, she managed to keep her baser instincts in line, but out here on the dirt roads of the Big Lonely, where what few vehicles there were could be seen from ten miles away, she pushed that car to its limits, just the way she'd always pushed her body. No, not quite as much: her body could do things that few other people in the world would even attempt.

And the old white Chevy, dented rear fender, broken grille and scraped door-panel attesting to the fact that Katie Barlow was still a better hurdler than she was a driver, was only a car. But it roared proudly along the dirt road, throwing back a wake of dust that would have suffocated Lawrence of Arabia. In the driver's seat, Katie was smiling, her teeth exposed like a filly's at the final turn of a stakes race. Another glance at the speedometer told her she was still doing close to eighty. It was not that knowledge, but the red-trimmed, rambling clapboard farmhouse half-a-mile ahead that made her ease off the accelerator. Her timing, as usual, was perfect: as she closed in on the mailbox at the end of the laneway she downshifted into second, swung the wheel sharply to the right, let the rear end follow in a ninety-degree arc, then dropped it into first and hit the gas pedal. The car responded, shooting up toward the Kornylo house and the now-visible farm buildings in a spray of gravel.

It was only when she saw Clare Kornylo come around the side of the house that Katie eased up; it wasn't that she felt ashamed or foolish or anything like that; it was just, well, older people sometimes got disturbed by things like that . . .

Not Clare, though. But by the time Katie remembered that, she was already parked and getting out of the car, and Clare, pushing at her red hair, trying to make herself presentable for whomever her visitor turned out to be, was coming around from the back of the house.

"Hey! Katie!" The smile arrived before the words. "It's been *so* long. When did you get back?"

"Last night. It's great to see you." She pushed the sunglasses back on her head in anticipation of the embrace that was to come. There weren't many people Katie Barlow loved more than Clare Kornylo, maybe nobody beyond her immediate family. And Katie? As corny as it sounded, Clare had always thought of Katie as a daughter and wasn't embarrassed to say so. It had only been a month since they'd last seen one another, but each checked out the other for changes. Clare, Katie thought, looked just a little more tired. Katie, Clare thought, looked better than she'd ever seen her.

"I tried the hospital again this morning," Katie said. "They said Aaron was home." She stopped and looked down. "I thought that maybe by now he'd be ready to see me." She'd been at the hospital when he'd come out of the anesthetic, and the day after when he was fully conscious. But he'd stared stubbornly at the wall, and when she'd asked him if he wanted her to stay, he'd said no, that he wanted to see nobody—not her, not his other friends, not even his family any more than he had to. "Do you think he'll want to see me now?" she asked.

"My guess is that he won't, Katie, at least not at

first. He's trying to work things out on his own, and it's hard to say just how far along he is." Then her voice brightened. "But *I* want to see you. We read all about Brazil in the papers. My, that must have been something!"

Katie was not quite listening. Instead she was peering over Clare's shoulder, trying not to be too obvious but failing.

"He's over in Willow Creek," Clare said, "seeing about some job. I'm expecting him back anytime. Now, are you going to tell me about Brazil or not?"

Ah, Brazil! The best few weeks of her life. In Munich she'd been nowhere, a 16-year-old, qualified but just tagging along for the trip more than anything else. Then nearly five years of finishing out of the precious metals in international competitions. Her best pentathlon ever came at Montreal, a fifth-place finish and a Canadian record but no medals. Then the gold at Edmonton, just like Aaron, in the Commonwealth Games. And then Brazil, where she pushed the American girl, Patty Dunlop, to her best performance ever and the fourth-best in the history of the event. And her point total, which bettered her own Canadian record, brought her the silver medal and renewed recognition as one of the best female athletes in the world. Brazil? Wonderful!

There was something else about Brazil too, but she didn't especially want to go into it with Clare, any more than she wanted to go into it with her own mother. Maybe that was the reason. Katie Barlow wasn't sure—and she tried not to say things she wasn't sure about—but she thought she had fallen just a little bit for somebody. She chose, instead, to attempt to dazzle Clare with enthusiasm.

"We're in the best shape we've ever been in. The team, I mean. Don't laugh, but we really might just wipe up in Moscow in eight, maybe twelve events. Maybe more, if we're lucky and they aren't."

Clare reached up to put her arm around Katie's shoulder, remembered she couldn't do that any more, and put it around her waist instead. As they walked to

the house, Katie said, very quietly: "I really didn't
think he'd be up and around yet." Clare didn't answer.
After all, it wasn't a real question.

Myles Kornylo stood a few feet back of the screen
door, sipping his black coffee and watching the exchange between Katie and Clare. It was not the first
time he'd admired Katie's fine young body, though he
most certainly never said so. Not that there was anything more to it than admiration, anyway; none of those
inner stirrings. No, Katie was like a daughter to him.
She'd only been . . . what?, ten?, no, eleven when her
family had moved to Willow Creek, where she'd met
Aaron and where their mutual love of track and field
had drawn them together. Although he never let on,
Myles would watch and smile as the two of them raced,
giggling and shouldering one another, up and down the
long drive, and hurdled the fences that surrounded
the farm buildings, and shinnied up the ropes in the
barn, swinging out and dropping happily into the hay.
He'd watched as their bodies developed and their minds
grew disciplined, winning everything in the district, then
the province. Then, as the competition increased, Aaron gave up both middle-distance running and the long
jump and concentrated fully on what he did best, the
high jump, and Katie, the more versatile of the two,
dropped everything but the pentathlon. He'd watched
them beat everybody else in the country and then give
the world a run for its money.

Myles had felt uncomfortable and out of place in
Montreal in '76: it was too big, too noisy, too filled
with too many people. It bothered him, as the father
of a challenger, that he could not get swept up in the
color and the pageantry of the parade, that the only
time he was touched by the national anthem was when
Aaron was on the dais, the bronze medal draped
around his neck. Patriotism was by and large lost on
him, and as far as athletic competition—sports—was
concerned, well that was for kids and people who could
afford it; he'd given all that up when he was seventeen.

No, he was there because Aaron was there. And

Katie, of course, but mostly Aaron. Oh God, how proud he'd been! It was funny, though: he could not remember actually screaming, or even—if the truth be known —seeing Aaron complete his jump. Maybe he'd turned his head away, maybe he couldn't look. But he did remember, so clearly, the first explosion of the crowd, like rolling thunder, and he could see Aaron, shooting up out of the mattresses, arms raised and fists clenched, laughing—yes, laughing—in pure unbridled joy.

"That was really something," he would tell his son later, when they had a few minutes alone together in Myles' and Clare's hotel room. There were so many other things he wanted to say—"I love you, son" was one of them—but he just couldn't. All he could say was: "That was really something."

"Your voice sounds funny, dad," Aaron had said. "Are you okay?"

"Yeah, it's probably a cold coming on. I'm not used to this damn air conditioning."

Now why did I go and say something like that? Myles was back in the present now, still behind the screen door. He berated himself a lot these days. Must be getting old, he thought, and turned his mind elsewhere. The coffee was getting cold, so he refilled the cup and stepped out into the yard.

While she had been able to call Clare by her Christian name without discomfort, Katie had never been able to do the same with Myles. And of course he had never invited her to do so. But when she saw him coming toward them, losing his battle with the sloshing coffee, she smiled a real smile and waved.

"You're looking a little more filled out," Myles said, his head cocked slightly to the side, the way it always was when he was embarrassed. "Fed you proper down there, did they?"

"Oh, you and my father. He said the same thing." Even when he was at his friendliest best, Myles was not an easy man for Katie to talk to. It may have been more her problem than his, but she was always afraid of saying the wrong thing, afraid that she would be the one responsible for putting him into a bad mood. Besides, her mind kept returning to the primary purpose of her mission to the Kornylo farm: Aaron.

"What's he doing in Willow Creek, anyway?" she asked them both.

"A job that's open at the high school," Clare said.

"You mean the counselor for the exercise program? I heard one of the Peterson girls already got it."

"That's fine," Myles said, meaning it. "Maybe that'll put an end to it."

There it is, Katie thought, the short fuse again, the thing about Myles that had always kept her uncomfortable, off balance. Somehow she'd expected—perhaps hoped was a better word—that the accident had changed him: after all it was his son and his harvester and he was driving it at the time. Her eyes flashed and then went dark. She could really hurt him here, she knew that, and she almost did. No, dammit, it wasn't his fault. She shook the demons out of her head and said, icily: "Anyway, that's what I heard. I don't think it was much of a job anyway."

"Maybe they were thinking of another job, Myles," Clare said, sensing the tension and trying to break it.

"And maybe they just wanted to see what he looks like," Myles replied, pretending to look directly at her but avoiding her eyes.

Katie couldn't let that one go unchallenged: "Aaron's got a lot of friends in athletics, Mr. Kornylo. Nobody'd hurt him."

But Myles wasn't listening any more. "This farm'll be his someday. Best for him if everybody kept that in mind." Myles didn't want to talk any more, and he especially didn't want to listen. These women, much as he loved them, could never understand. Katie and Clare had long since broken him of the habit of saying things like "man's talk" and "man's work" but they could not break his habit of thinking that way. He had worked this farm the way his father had before him, and the way his father's father had worked the land back in the Ukraine. When he was dead, or too old or too sick, Aaron would have the farm. That is what the Kornylo men did. Period. He stomped off toward the barn; then, remembering the broken plough hitch, he changed direction and picked up the welding mask.

Katie was counting on Clare to get the two of them out of this awkward moment and, as usual, Clare came through.

"So . . . you're going to start training for Moscow soon, I suppose?"

"I've got to get ready for the trials in September, first. In Vancouver. Then, hopefully, for Moscow. I'll probably leave next week."

The change in Clare's expression was totally unexpected. It wasn't Katie's imagination either, because the tone of voice—an imploring quality Katie had never heard before and didn't like—confirmed it. "Can't you train in town?" Clare asked. "I was kind of hoping you'd spend a little time . . . here."

Okay, Katie Barlow, how are you going to respond to this? Are you going to tell her *all* about Brazil, about Greg, about the things you felt then and are still feeling now? No. She'll guess, probably. "One of our teammates . . . Aaron knows him . . . in fact, you've met him . . . Greg Dubois . . . he invited me to come down to his family's place just outside Montreal. We were going to train together."

"Well, you couldn't pass that up," Clare said, a little too enthusiastically.

"Right!" Also too enthusiastically. In the long pause that followed, Katie started looking around for something to look at. The dust trail along the southern horizon was, she was certain, Aaron's. As she watched it come closer, a thought entered her mind: How could Aaron drive without his right leg?

But before she could ask the question, Clare answered it: "When he was getting ready to come home from the hospital," she said. "Myles took the car in and had them switch the gas pedal over to the left side like they do. It's automatic so everything else was okay. It was kind of a coming-home present."

• • •

When Aaron saw Katie's car, his temper, already simmering from the rejection he'd just received (oh, the son of a bitch had tried to be nice, but . . .) went suddenly up to a boil. What the hell was she doing here? Hadn't he told her to stay away from him? Didn't she know how much she reminded him of so many things, things that he had to forget for his own good? What did she want, anyway? To see for herself how deformed he was, how clumsy?

He parked as far from the two women as he could, over by the green toolshed, so that if he muffed his exit, as he had done when he got out to go into the school earlier that morning, they wouldn't see it. He pulled the crutches from the passenger's side, lined them up parallel at arm's length, and tried to pull himself up onto them. The right crutch slipped and he went down, cursing quietly. Katie and Clare, watching Aaron's performance, saw him disappear beneath the car windows, then come up again in full stride, jerking his body along. They couldn't see his face, though, which was crimson with shame and frustration, and therefore they couldn't see his lip, which he'd bitten half-through in his anger.

Inside the toolshed, Aaron slapped at the door with his elbow, hoping it would slam closed. But the hinges were old and rusted, and it creaked only part way. No matter. He looked up at the hanging bare bulb, reached up for the chain, then changed his mind. There was enough light coming through the window. Setting his left crutch against a sawhorse, Aaron pulled back the green tarp to reveal an almost-finished canoe. This had been last winter's project, something to fill in those long nights and short days when the land lay under blowing snow. It was something to do when the roads were filled in and he couldn't get into Willow Creek District High to jump, jump, jump until his body almost screamed for him to stop. When the spring came, early for a change, he had pulled the tarp over the canoe and left it. Then there was the accident.

He tried to remember what turned him on to canoe-

ing. Oh yeh, it was at Greg's place, up in the Laurentians, where he and Katie had gone after the Olympics
to rest, to come down. Greg, when he was a few years
younger, had done some white-water stuff, and he had a
couple of racing canoes up at the summer home. Aaron
remembered the two of them, Greg and Katie, out on
the lake, laughing and shouting at one another as Greg
gave her his "crash course." For all he liked Greg,
and despite the fact that Katie was never officially "his
girl," Aaron had felt jealousy pangs high in his belly.
So he decided he should have that crash course too, and
although he never came close to matching Greg's style
and grace, he did, with sheer determination, finally
beat him in a cross-the-lake race. It was a bigger kick
than topping Greg in the high jump, which he did
with regularity.

At that very moment Aaron was not all that interested in the canoe; he was only interested in not seeing
Katie. It was foolish, he knew, because she would come
in—but he was damned if he was going to encourage
her. Behind him he heard the door creak full open, and
heard the click as the light came on. He felt a strong
grip on his right shoulder, a light one on the left:
she was turning him around to face her. He felt her
light kiss on his now-swollen lips. Still, he would not
look at her; he kept his eyes down and waited until
she relaxed her hold, then he turned back to the canoe,
searching almost desperately for a spot that needed
sanding.

"It's been a long time, Aaron."

No reply.

"I tried to see you at the hospital." It was unlike her,
Aaron thought, not to come right out with it, to de-
mand to know why he had refused to see her. More
than anybody he knew, Katie Barlow had always main-
tained that the closest distance between two people, for
good or ill, was a straight line. As recently as last summer, at Edmonton, he'd taken a punch in the nose for
her trouble, when she told some redneck in a bar that
"Alberta sucked." Funny, but the sudden recollection

of that was softening his edges. It had been a good fight, if a short one. But boy, if he ever saw that guy again, he'd . . . hit him with his crutch.

"Why are you laughing?" Katie demanded. It wasn't that she didn't like it, it was just that it was unexpected.

The mood was fragile and it cracked. "Nothing. Just something I remembered." Then, more softly: "I didn't want to see anybody at the hospital, that's all. Not even my parents. I just didn't want anybody to see me like . . . like this."

"I was hurt, you know."

"You'd have been hurt worse if you'd seen me." When he first saw her car, when he first saw her, when she came into the shed, the only thought in his mind was getting rid of her, getting her out of there. He did not want to listen to one of her lectures, or hear about how great it had been in Brazil or any of those things. Maybe what he'd least wanted to find out was that she still cared about him, loved him in that special way. Didn't she know he was no longer what she thought he was?

"I never did hear exactly how it happened," Katie said.

"How what happened?" Aaron needed a few seconds to get out of his reverie. "I don't remember it very clearly . . . I was shoveling the grain and the thing caught in my boot. I remember hearing a scream—and it was me—and I remember dad bending over me, prying with a bar. Funny, but it didn't hurt then, I couldn't feel anything. I couldn't see dad all that well, there was this whitish light all around, like in my peripheral vision, you know. And I guess I asked him if my boot was wrecked—at least he said I did—'cause the boots were new and I was worried I'd ruined them. It's really amazing how in just a second . . ."

He was going to tell her about the dream too, but it really wouldn't have added anything. She'd have assured him it would go away, and he'd have mumbled agreement, and she'd have talked about some bad recurring dream she'd once had and so on. Some other time, maybe.

"I went to see about a job today," Aaron said instead, following up the words with an almost-smile and the universal thumbs-down gesture of failure.

"Yes, I know. But don't worry Aaron, there'll be other jobs. And anyway, there's always the farm."

This time Aaron's mood didn't crack. It shattered. "You've been talking to my father!"

"Aaron, I . . ."

"Never mind your goddamned 'Aaron, I!' What'd he do, send you in here to soften me up, to give me a good talking-to?"

Katie's black Cree eyes flashed, and she yanked her hand off his arm even before he remembered it was there and pulled away himself.

"Damn you Aaron, you know better than that. I don't carry anybody's messages. It was an alternative, that's all. And if I offended you, well that's too damned bad. Maybe that skin of yours is a little too thin for your own good." This wasn't working at all. She took a deep breath and reached for him again.

"Thanks for stopping by," he said coldly, picking up a piece of two-by-four and measuring it across the canoe's gunwales.

"Are you dismissing me?" Katie asked, the coldness in her own voice matching his, degree by falling degree.

"I'm just sick of this thing sitting here unfinished, that's all."

Katie whirled to leave, but she got only as far as the door. After all, she had come there expecting the worst from him and had tried to rehearse for it. Under the circumstances, in this particular clash of egos, she was prepared to sacrifice hers to his. She walked up behind him and began kneading his shoulders, just the way she'd always done, just the way he liked it. "Aaron . . ."

He turned on her, his face red and clenched like a fist. He jabbed his thumb into his chest and shouted, spitting the words into her face.

"Hey lady, remember me? I was going to take the Gold in Moscow. *Remember?* Now I'm not good enough to nursemaid a bunch of kids . . . College coaches don't even want to know if I'm still alive, and my old man wants to plant me here like one of his vegetables. Go on! Go on, get out of here! Just leave me alone for a while, okay?"

She opened her mouth to answer, to tell him what a child he was being, then thought the better of it. Instead she turned on her heel (if he could be histrionic, so could she) and huffed out. Her attempt to punctuate her exit with a door-slamming failed: the old stiff hinges just creaked once more and held their ground.

Aaron shoved the two-by-four into the vice and gave the handle a too-powerful twist. The metal jaws crunched into the wood, not ruining it, but, in Aaron's mind at that time, negating all the careful work he'd put into the rest of the canoe. Well, the hell with it, it was just a dumb canoe anyway! But his anger had about doubled and it was showing no signs of reversing itself.

Then the pain came, in the ankle that wasn't there.

The doctors had warned him this might happen, that he might suffer from what they called "phantom limb syndrome." They'd explained that the nerves that carried messages from his foot and lower leg, while truncated, retained their capacities to transmit. They said if he was really lucky he wouldn't have it, but very probably he would experience this eerie pain from time to time. This was the first and it was fierce: light patterns began to develop before his eyes; sweat broke out on his forehead and upper lip; he wanted to holler but instead he grunted, reaching down instinctively to rub at the stump through his jeans. That helped. Though it was still there, at least the pain was no longer unbearable. He turned back to his two-by-four.

Aaron picked up the saw, a short and inflexible type used for fine cuts and mitering. He looked for his pencil-mark guide on the wood, then realized that in his rush of anger, he hadn't made one. But the idea of taking the wood out of the vice again, measuring it up and marking it was not a palatable one just then. He guessed at the angle and started to cut. Then the pain in his leg came back and his hand jerked. The saw ran down the two-by-four, scraped across the webbing between thumb and forefinger of his left hand, and gouged into the back of his wrist. "Goddammit!" he shouted, flinging the saw across the small room, as far from him as he could get it. He reached down and turned the handle of the vice harder and harder until the sweat seared his eyes and bile rose in his throat, until the wood crunched and splintered. "Good!" he said. "Good!"

The blood was running profusely, and as the throbbing in his leg began to disappear, the pain in his wrist grew. He was beginning to feel a little foolish, partly about Katie and partly about the idiot performance he'd just given for himself alone; but under the circumstances that only made him angrier. There was a greasy, dirty old rag on the work bench and he picked it up, rubbing away as much of the blood as he could, scrubbing at the wound to make it hurt all the more, to atone for his stupidity.

It helped. After a few moments he had calmed down enough to realize that some medical attention was in order. He carefully wrapped the rag around his wrist, tucking the ends underneath to secure it, climbed onto his crutches and headed toward the house.

If Clare had known what was going on, she'd have tried to do something about it, even if it was nothing more than intercepting Katie in the yard and reassuring her. But by the time she realized that all was not well —by way of the slamming door and the floored engine and the spray of gravel hitting the house—Katie was already a speeding dust-storm heading toward the horizon. In half an hour or so Clare would try to call her at home, because one thing was coming clear: she needed that girl, or at least Aaron did. There were things a mother could give, but they had limits. A mother couldn't push the way a friend could, couldn't offer advice when none was asked for; and she couldn't make the pain go away with a kiss and a cookie—not any more.

As she put away the last of the bedding she heard the water being turned on in the kitchen, and a muttered word that sounded very much like "shit." She found Aaron standing there, grimacing as the hot water ran over and into the gash on his wrist. In his right hand he was rolling a bar of yellow Sunlight soap around and around, working up a lather.

Just as he was about to apply it, Clare was beside him, reaching for his damaged hand. "Here, let me see that." Aaron instinctively tried to pull away, but his heart wasn't in it. He proffered his hand for his mother's inspection, while assuring her that "it's all right."

"Now just stand still!" Clare said. How many times in the last twenty-odd years had she stood there with him at the sink, tending to one scrape or scratch or cut or another? "It's just a bad habit that comes from being a mother," she tried to explain.

Holding the hand out over the sink, she poured hydrogen peroxide over it liberally. It stung, as it always did, and Aaron winced, as he always did. Then, having soaked a cotton ball in the antiseptic, she dabbed away the last of the dirt. The blood flow was decreasing now, but there was still enough to soak through the gauze strip she wound carefully around the hand and wrist.

"What happened?" Myles, standing in the doorway, had just caught the tail end of the operation. He saw the blood, his son's blood, and was seized by a terrible memory, of that same blood seeping out of a mangled boot, disappearing forever into the soil.

"He's all right," Clare assured.

"An accident," Aaron added.

Myles was only half-listening. In a few long strides he was in front of Aaron, demanding that he have a chance to decide for himself if it was really "all right."

"Let's see," he said, reaching out. Once again an honest emotion—concern, this time—was showing itself as anger.

"It's okay!" Aaron said, pulling back.

For a few long seconds father and son were eye-to-eye. It was Myles who finally backed off.

But he couldn't let it go: "Maybe," he said, halfway into his turn, "you'd better keep away from the tools until you can handle them better."

Aaron wanted to reply. He wanted to say, "Damn you," more than just about anything, but the words stuck in his throat; he simply couldn't say them in front of his parents, much less *to* them, not since the time when he was seven or eight and, in all innocence, he'd repeated, at the supper table, the phrase he'd just picked up in the school yard. His father had hauled him out to the toolshed for a pants-down spanking and a warning that, if he ever heard that kind of talk from his son again, it would be the razor strop, not just his hand. Later, when he was in bed, his mother had come in, pushed the blond curls away from his forehead, taken his hand, and explained in detail what he had quite innocently said, and where it came from, and why it was wrong to use it—all in terms that a kid could understand.

So Aaron stifled himself. He just glared at the back of his father's head, jammed the crutches under his armpits and swung himself out of the kitchen. He was still going to work on that bloody canoe.

Clare walked around in front of her husband, absently screwing the cap back on the disinfectant.

"Myles," she began, "he can manage . . ."

Myles was caught somewhere between moods. The anger hadn't quite subsided and the contrition hadn't quite taken over. Finally, softly: "Is he all right?"

"I don't think it'll need stitches."

"Well, that's good." Out in the yard, Aaron abruptly changed direction and started propelling himself around the side of the house. As Myles watched he said, mostly to himself: "Wonder why he doesn't wear that false leg?"

"Says it bothers him," Clare replied. "Says it hurts when he puts his weight on it. Says it's like dragging something dead around."

"When did he tell you all this?" Myles was getting irritated again, irritated at the thought that his wife knew things about Aaron's "condition" that he didn't.

"The other day. I asked him. Sit, I'll make you some coffee."

Aaron went in by the front door this time, the one rarely used, except by certain guests—which meant, by and large, the doctor and the minister. He was in no mood to see either of his parents at that moment, and in no mood to have them see him. With both crutches under his right arm for balance he pulled himself upstairs on the banister. He entered his room and closed the door quietly, and for a long time he lay on the newly-made bed, his bandaged hand flung across his eyes. He tried to come down, to relax, to sleep if he could. He made himself breathe deeply. He attempted to think of happy times—"perfect moments" as an aunt of his once described them—and lose himself for as long as he could. But he couldn't lose himself at all: the most perfect moment of his life, the one that intruded on mountain sunsets and moonlit winter evenings, even that first, frightening, thrilling love-making on the soft grass of the creek banks, was looking up at that crossbar, seven feet and six-and-a-half inches above the ground and hearing the swelling roar of the crowd. And that was a magic moment he had to extinguish, not kindle, because he knew, lying there, that he could never look up at another crossbar, never hear that applause again.

Aaron sat up abruptly and just looked at the wall, at the photograph of him, medal hanging around his neck, standing just to the left and just below the East German who'd topped him by an inch. He let his eyes trail over the other photos and citations and medals, and the trophies on the shelf. His eyes stopped at the Olympic bronze. When he forced them away he found himself looking at that damned wooden leg. Then he was looking at both, alternately.

2

It was an old, quiet house on a silent summer night, and the first splintering of wood and glass sounded like an explosion. Myles was out of his chair so fast that the kitchen table had risen part of the way with him. Clare almost lost the coffee pot she was carrying from the stove to refill her husband's empty cup, but she righted it in time. Two pairs of eyes went instinctively to the ceiling. There was another crash, followed by a third and a fourth. Five! Six! Seven! They stopped counting. Clare reached out for Myles' hand and together they stood there, in the middle of the kitchen, knowing now exactly what was happening. Myles pulled his hand free and started toward the door. "Don't!" Clare commanded. He stopped. Before he could start again she was in front of him, blocking his path. "Let him . . ." Myles had had every intention of pushing around her, and it wasn't her words that stopped him. It was her eyes. They froze him. "Let's go out for a walk around the yard," she said, taking his hand once again.

Aaron stood, his elbows resting on the high dresser, supporting his weight. His chest was heaving, his mouth was dry and his eyes were wet. He surveyed his handiwork: every piece of glass was shattered, every frame broken, every display case wrecked, every photo and citation torn. What was left of the wall was bare, save for a few lonely nails. The Bronze was nowhere to be

25

seen: under the bed, maybe; who cared? The prosthesis was still in his right hand, scarred and glistening in spots where slivers of glass had embedded themselves, but not much the worse for wear. The damn thing was mocking him. He flung it at the wall, tearing out another chunk of wallpaper and plaster. Then he went back to the bed, brushed off the debris that had landed there, and lay down again.

But the longer he lay there, the more foolish he felt. And the more foolish he felt, the angrier he became. Instead of dissipating the black impotent fury, he had managed to increase it. The dynamite had not gone off, only the blasting cap.

There was something in him that he had to exorcise, something he had childishly hoped would be driven out when he beat and crushed the reminders of his past with the reminder of his present. In the past, when these feelings came, he'd burned them off, running and jumping and pumping iron until his body was too weary in that good-pain way to accommodate them further. But this body he had now . . . what could it do?

The dark thoughts began to converge, and when they formed their pattern, Aaron was not even shocked by it: it was true that at that very moment he didn't much care whether he lived or died. Everything was behind him anyway. He'd had his future. Besides, he was luckier than most people: he'd left a legacy. Scattered all over the floor.

There were no sounds in the house, save his own breathing and the incessant pounding of blood in his right temple. What were his parents doing, anyway? Why hadn't they come up, stopped him, calmed him down, held him like they had all those years ago?

He listened again at the head of the stairs. Nothing. He descended gingerly, waiting to hear his name called with a question mark after it. He was alone, finally, in the kitchen, where the unwashed dishes were still on the table and beside the sink, and the pots of potatoes and carrots were growing stone cold on the stove. Then he saw them, silhouetted against the ball of setting sun that was just touching the earth. They were walking away from him, toward the rise where sundown lasted those few precious moments longer, hand-in-hand. Another time such affection would have moved him.

But his only thoughts were dark and mean and angry, and filtering through all of them was the overwhelming need to get away from there, as fast as he could, someplace where there were no walls for his feelings to bounce off of, and come back redoubled.

He pushed through the screen door and swung around the side of the house to the toolshed. The canoe wasn't quite finished, but it was probably seaworthy, and if it wasn't, well, he'd find that out in the morning.

Myles and Clare, mostly at her gentle insistence, stayed out on the rise well into the darkiness, watching until the last ribbon of light had dripped off the last stringy cloud in the western sky. The topic of Aaron came up only once, much earlier, and they agreed that if he didn't come to them in the morning, then they would go to him. They also agreed that things could not go on this way much longer. Neither said it, because they were not the kind of people who felt comfortable with the idea, but both were thinking about, maybe, a psychiatrist.

The house was as silent as they'd left it.

Myles waited until the sounds in the kitchen assured him that Clare was, for the next fifteen or twenty minutes, busy with the dishes. Yes, he had promised to do nothing until morning, but he simply couldn't wait, that's all. Uncharacteristically he stole up the stairs, walking on the side nearest the wall, where the steps didn't squeak.

"Aaron?" He questioned the darkened room. "Aaron?" Glass scrunched under his feet and as his eyes accustomed themselves he began to see the devastation.

The window was open and he went to it. In the light of the half moon, he could see Aaron below, doing something with his car. It took a few more blinks before he could see exactly what. It was the canoe! Aaron was tying the canoe to the roof of the car. "Hey!" He saw

Aaron turn toward him, and felt their eyes lock in the darkness. Then, without further acknowledgement, Aaron was adjusting the ropes, his back to the window and the man standing in it.

By the time Myles was downstairs, out the door, and turning the corner of the house, the Dodge's big engine was exploding to life. By the time he reached the car it was already moving, slowly and deliberately. Myles caught one glimpse of the face behind the wheel, and for a second or so it stopped him. It was Aaron all right, but not any Aaron he'd ever known.

"Myles!" Clare had caught up with her husband. "Myles, what's going on here? Where's he going?"

"Crazy goddamn kid. I don't know. He's got the bloody canoe. I don't know but I'll bloody well find out."

"No!"

"Get out of my way, Clare."

"Wait!"

"I don't have time to play games with him," Myles said, still more to himself than Clare or anyone else. The door of his truck was open now and he was pulling on the big woolen plaid work shirt he kept on the seat.

"You can't haul him back here like a child," Clare shouted. "You've got to try to help him work it out for himself."

"For how long?" he yelled back. "For how long?"

"However long it takes."

Aaron's taillights were still visible in the distance, and would be for a few miles yet. Out on the prairie there's not much around to block the view.

Myles climbed into the truck, opened the choke halfway, and turned the key. From the porch Clare watched the second set of taillights begin their pursuit of the first.

3

The water ran black and impassively by, hardly disturbing the reflected light of the half moon. Aaron, sitting up against the overturned canoe, his lower body wrapped in the sleeping bag against the late evening chill, was not watching. His eyes were closed, his arms folded in front of his chest. For the benefit of his father, who Aaron knew was standing high on the bank above, he pretended to be sleeping.

But he was listening, listening to the only sound to disturb the prairie night—and it didn't disturb, really; in fact, it complemented, and enhanced.

The rapids. Aaron let his mind drift downstream a mile, and back in time a dozen years. The rapids had been his secret place. He would beg a picnic lunch from his mother, pack it carefully in his little knapsack, and ride off down the road on his bicycle to spend the day on his very own grey-sand beach, whittling a little, fishing a little, but mostly just watching the water churn by. He'd loved to see the water hit the rocks, rise into that fine white spray that turned golden when the afternoon sun was just right, then crash back down into its own blackness. And he'd loved that sound, the one he was so intently listening to now, the sound of wild natural power, always changing its nuance, but never diminishing (except during the spring run-off, of course, when the rapids weren't there at all).

Then one day, not long after his thirteenth birthday,

his father, putting down the telephone, announced:
"There's trouble over by the rapids. Some kids. Got to
get over there." Aaron, insistent, tagged along; and
when they'd reached the bank they'd seen Mr. Ellison
coming up carrying something in a blanket. Mr. Ellison had been crying, and had passed them without
even noticing, walking jerkily toward the old town am-
bulance. Aaron had started to speak but his father
stopped him with a shake of the head. On Aaron's little
beach were shards of a broken rowboat.

Across the water some other men and been standing
over another small shape covered by a blanket. After
that day Aaron had not returned to his rapids much.
And when he did it somehow wasn't the same.

Myles stood on the bank above Aaron for a long
time, an hour maybe. He knew that Aaron knew he
was there—couldn't have missed the sound of the ag-
ing pickup, not in all that silence—and he knew that
the likelihood of his son acknowledging his presence
was pretty slim. But he waited and he watched until
finally Aaron slid all the way down in his sleeping bag
and, as the fire died, went off to sleep. Myles climbed
back into the truck, wrapped himself in the old blue-
and-green plaid blanket he kept behind the seat and,
despite all efforts, nodded off himself.

Aaron got up with the birds. Stars were still visible
in the eastern sky, but the blackness was dissolving
into a bluish grey. One solitary elongated cloud, far,
far away, reflected the first golden glow of morning
light. A fish broke the surface of the water, then another. The birds yammered their wake-up calls to one another, and, on this particular morning, to Aaron Kornylo. His body ached from the hard sand and the morning
dampness; the stump was throbbing, but that pain was
no worse than the one across the back of his shoulders,
which was to say, not too bad at all.

After a few moments of shuddering and flexing he
wriggled out of the sleeping bag, got the crutches under
himself, and stood. He refused to look up behind him;

he knew his father was still there. In fact, in a perverse way he was glad. If there hadn't been an audience, he might have changed his mind. An audience made the whole thing so much more clear-cut. He was especially glad the audience was his father.

It was time. He righted the canoe, put in the paddle, stood his crutches against an outcropping and then, on hands and knee, pushed the canoe to the water's edge.

When Myles awoke the canoe was already in the water and Aaron, paddling easily and (to Myles' uncritical eye) rhythmically, was steering it into the first bend. He had disappeared by the time Myles was down the bank, standing over the remnants of the campfire. "Aaron!" he shouted, knowing that even if his son could have heard him it wouldn't have made any difference. This was not supposed to happen—not the way Myles had figured it the night before. What was supposed to happen was that Aaron would sleep off his snit, pack up and come home—as he always used to do when he ran away from home. Grabbing the crutches, the sleeping bag and—Oh, Jesus God—the orange life jacket, Myles scrambled back up the hill to the truck. "Please God," he prayed, "please let it start!"

The river grew shallower and the banks began to close in. The foliage on either side was little more than one dark blur, broken only occasionally by tiny explosions of light as the rising sun intruded itself. Aaron, his upper body straight up, just the way Greg had taught him, was feathering the water now, steering only, paddling only for position; the current was so swift there was no other option. He was getting the feeling now, emptying his mind, letting his body and his instincts take over. It hadn't happened for a long time, not since the last jump: how often he had tried to make it happen, lying there in that hospital bed, and then again at home, but there had been some block; there was just no way.

It was, however, happening now. His eyes unfocused and suddenly he was really *seeing*—seeing but not consciously acknowledging. Despite the speed, the world was slowing down; messages were bypassing the brain, going directly to the powerful arms and chest and gut. Faster, faster. Slower, slower. Aaron saw the rapids approaching and the paddle was involuntarily pulled across his body, the water stirred, the direction changed. His body had easily found the channel, easily avoided the first great smooth rock. And the second. And . . .

The river is not mocked. In a battle of sheer strength, the river always wins.

From high above, Myles saw the canoe turn sideways, saw Aaron hurled out into the exploding current, all in that inexorable slow motion that for some reason people experience as tragedies unfold. The canoe bounced along the rocks, into the water, out again. It might as well have been a toy which, from where Myles sat, it resembled. Aaron had not surfaced! Myles released the clutch and, praying out loud without even realizing it, tore off down the dirt road that continued to parallel the river bank.

Within thirty seconds he was jumping and sliding down the bank, to the spot where the Ellison boy and his cousin had been found, to Aaron's special place. The turbulence was diminished here, though that wasn't saying very much. Myles, paddle and life jacket in hand, tied one end of the rope he carried to a tree trunk, the other around his waist. Then he stood on the water's edge, waiting.

Aaron's paddle came first, went straight up in an eddy, then settled between two rocks. The river grabbed it again and it disappeared downstream. The canoe followed, half full of water and not bouncing any more. Out of the corner of his eye—his attention was elsewhere; upstream—Myles saw the canoe slide halfway up the grey beach on the opposite side and anchor there under its own weight. But there was no Aaron. Instinctively, Myles began running along the bank, forgetting the rope around his waist. There was an "ummph" and he went down; but as he fell he saw an arm come out of the water. Then a head, its mouth open, spitting water and sucking for air at the same time. The head went under again . . . five seconds . . . ten seconds . . . fifteen! "Oh, please God! . . ."

Aaron resurfaced directly across the river, got his arms around a rock, and hung there. For better or for worse, he'd made it. He could not let himself slip back into that water, as easy as that would have been: relax the grip and it would suck him away. After a few more seconds, coughing and spluttering, he pulled himself up a little higher, lay his face on the water-smoothed surface, closed his eyes and pulled air into his lungs, as much and as quickly as he could manage. In a short time his athlete's body had replenished itself, and the breathing process returned to normal. Then and only then did Aaron look up. He and his father stared at one another. Almost curiously. Almost as if they were seeing one another for the first time. Neither spoke.

Aaron was the first to look away and when he did he saw the canoe, no more than fifteen feet from him. Pulling himself from rock to rock, staying out of the main current, he reached it, came up to a sitting position beside it, and, with some effort, turned it over, dumping the water, all save an inch or so in the bottom. He couldn't see any holes or tears and, by turning the canoe to one side and then the other, sloshing the water, he satisfied himself that it was still whole and seaworthy; then he drained it completely. When he next looked at his father, Myles was standing in exactly the same spot, extra paddle in one hand and lifejacket in the other. To Aaron's eye, his father seemed planted there; he had not seen the shoulders fall or heard the expulsion of breath that Myles had been holding—it felt like forever—in his lungs.

Myles flipped the paddle across. He swung the life jacket over his head and released it. It fluttered down about five feet to Aaron's left. Then Myles turned and hauled himself back up to the truck. Aaron listened to the door shut and the engine come alive. He listened to the gears change and the muffler complain. He listened until there was no sound at all, save the rushing water and his own quiet breathing.

Then he put the canoe back in the water, retrieved the extra paddle, and started to climb in. For a second he hesitated, then picked up the life jacket and put it on. There was no longer any reason not to wear it. He was quite certain of that now.

4

Katie wasn't at all sure she wanted to be anywhere near the Kornylo farm that afternoon, or any future afternoon. The old white Chevy had never moved quite so slowly under her administration before, and the closer she got, the less pressure she applied to the gas pedal. If Clare hadn't called that morning and asked her to come over, Katie would probably not have made the trip. It wasn't as if she thought she could do any good, despite what Clare had said. Aaron may have needed a friend, but Aaron didn't seem to be able to handle a friend.

As much as Katie told herself that she didn't believe in obligation, she knew she really did. She owed Aaron for a lot of happiness, and a lot of support when the world got a little too tough for her. Clare too, for that matter. Nothing memorable, just little things. But important things. And she loved these people. Besides, giving up was a foreign concept to her: nobody got where she was in athletics, with its pain and its disappointments, without single-mindedness bordering on compulsion. She'd seen too many people quit "just for this one time" and then start drifting away for good. Talented people, too: natural athletes; better than she was.

Aaron might well be beyond her reach, but in the few days she had before taking off for Montreal and Greg, she was going to give it her best shot.

The canoe stood against the shed, and Katie could see before she was out of the car that there was something frighteningly different about it. As she walked closer to inspect it she ran into Myles, who was coming around the barn with a bundle of empty feed sacks on his shoulder.

"Where's Aaron?" she asked, her eyes still on the canoe.

"Inside. Having a nap, I think. The boy had a long night. Just got in a little while ago."

Katie didn't hear the last sentence. She was already asking, "How did this happen?" She was having visions of Aaron, like that guy in the *Walking Tall* movie they'd seen together, out here in the middle of the night pounding away at the canoe with a baseball bat or something. That's what it looked like.

"Tried to shoot the rapids," Myles explained matter-of-factly. "Scuffed a few rocks. He's fine." He dropped the sacks and joined her beside the canoe and ran his fingers along one of the more prominent gashes. "Scuffed *quite a few* rocks, it appears."

If Myles thought this was funny—and he seemed to be enjoying it—Katie did not. In fact, she was feeling just mean enough to take on the Myles Kornylo anger that afternoon, and she came very close to precipitating it. But she held off: probably nothing she could say would make him see Aaron's escapade any differently anyway.

"Where did he try?" she asked instead.

"Down off the southeast section," Myles replied, that hint of what she was defining as macho pride still in his voice.

"He shot *those* rapids?" She knew about *those* rapids. She knew about the Ellison boy, and the other boy with him. The whole school had gone to the funeral.

"He won't try it again for a while, I promise you that," Myles said, picking up the grain sacks and moving away from her, toward the truck. Then, as a teasing exit line, he talked to her over his shoulder: "Not without a life jacket, anyway."

The color drained from her face. Not . . . without
. . . a life jacket? It was even worse than she'd thought.
How could that man be smiling about it? Didn't the
damn fool know that his son might have killed himself,
might even have been trying to kill himself? But she'd
tackle Myles Kornylo some other time—if there turned
out to be another time. It was his goddamned crazy
son she had come to see, and now she had more reason than ever.

She found Aaron at the kitchen table, cleaning up
the last of the egg yolk on his plate with a slab of
bread. He was smiling. He was happy . . . and, apparently, happy to see her. For the moment, she was dis-
armed. So he *was* okay. Fine. What she had to say
could wait a few minutes.

"I want to talk to you," Katie said.

"So talk."

"I think we should take a walk—if you're up to it."

"Sure," he said, climbing onto his crutches. "Any
particular direction?"

The seeds of an attack plan were beginning to ges-
tate in her mind. "Let's go down around the swimming
hole." He followed her out the door.

Aaron seemed absolutely jaunty as they strolled
along the river bank, miles upstream from the rapids.
It was going to be a shame to bring him down, but it
had to be done. He couldn't go through his life hopping back and forth between self-pity and mindless
heroics. Or maybe he could, but if he did, she wouldn't
be around to see it. If she contributed nothing further to
their relationship, she was going to snap him back to
reality, at least this time.

"You should have called me," she said.

"Well," Aaron said, "I sort of wanted to do it myself."

"The canoe got kind of battered up."

"Yeah . . ." He was getting some idea of where the
conversation was going.

"*Why* did you try?" She was attempting to read his

face, but right then she might as well have been talking to Myles. Nothing.

"To see if I could make it." If she was going to get anything out of him, she'd have to drag it out. It wasn't that he felt angry with her or anything like that: he just didn't have the answers himself yet, so he didn't have them to give her.

"But you didn't make it. The canoe tipped."

"Yeah," Aaron allowed himself a Gary Cooper kind of smile, "but *I* still made it." He was standing with his back to the river. Behind him an old rope and tire hung from the heavy willow branch, as it had for as long as either of them could remember.

Okay, she'd planned for a different defense on his part but she could handle this one. "Must have been your strong swimming style," Katie said sarcastically. "Why don't you demonstrate for me?" With that she grabbed the crutches, raised her right leg, and shoved him backward into the river.

"No, I . . ." Aaron protested—futilely, since he was in mid-flight at the time.

"Sure, let's see," Katie smiled as his body hit the water butt-first.

"Katie!"

"Oh, I see. You've lost your taste for water. You can't swim. You never could. Is that it?" She threw the crutches aside, folded her arms across her chest and spread her legs slightly in that universal stance of defiance. "Is that it, Aaron?"

"Hey Katie, come on!" Aaron was thrashing the water with his arms, trying to find bottom with his left foot. But it was deep here; this was where the other kids used to skinny-dip, to dive from the willow limb, to swing out on the rope-and-tire and drop into the natural pool. The knowledge that Katie would not let him drown was, at that point, small comfort. For the second time that day Aaron was spitting out water. "Katie," he glubbed, "please!"

"*Sure* you can," Katie sneered, her voice growing colder, her words measured for effect.

"I can't . . ." he admitted, thrashing toward the

bank. She retrieved one of the crutches and jabbed it at him, forcing him back. Somehow he made his way to the tire, reached up and held on with both hands. He looked up at her sheepishly, but she had not changed her position or her expression. He thought of brutal matrons in the old prison movies he'd seen on TV. Finally she sat—still glaring but at least sitting. He let go of the tire and, with as much dignity as he could conjure up under the circumstances, paddled doggie-fashion toward her.

"Enough's enough, Katie," he said with just a touch of whine in his voice.

She jabbed him back with the menacing crutch. "I'll be the judge of that." Then: "Stand up."

"Stand up?"

"Yes. Stand up, dammit! STAND UP!"

She walked around in little circles, forming the phrases in her head. What was the matter with him? Didn't he realize what he'd done? Why did he insist on making a joke of it now?

"Aaron," she said finally, "you could have died out there this morning. No, don't pretend to look shocked. You could have died and you know it."

"I could die right here."

"Shut up, goddamn you, this isn't funny. This isn't a joke. And if you're feeling so good about yourself right now, well I can tell you it's not going to last."

Sensing—rightly—that she would not push him back this time, he pushed and paddled through the water until it was shallow enough to sit. He was close enough to see the tears on her cheeks.

"Katie . . ." Maybe if he just let the words come out they'd make some sense. "Katie, I just knew last night I had to do something. I mean, I smashed all my trophies and prizes and stuff and that only made things worse. I don't know what else I thought, but I thought I was exploding. I did what I had to do, and . . ."

"Bullshit!"

"But . . ."

"Bullshit! Come on, Aaron, you're not a child even if you insist on acting like one. You know about those rapids. You knew that canoe hadn't even been tested in the water before. You knew you left your life jacket behind. You weren't just working off tension, you were putting your life in danger. Just who the hell do you think you are, Aaron Kornylo?"

"You could be wrong, you know," he said quietly. It wasn't a challenge. He was in no position to challenge her, physically or intellectually.

"Am I, Aaron?" she sobbed. "Am I?"

After a long pause, he answered. "No, no you're not wrong. But I never actually said to myself that I was going to kill myself. I think I knew it was possible . . ."

"Probable!"

"Okay, probable. But last night, when I left the house, and then again this morning when I put the canoe in the river, well, I guess somewhere inside I must have known. I know I looked at that life jacket, and I was going to put it on, and then I didn't. I can't explain it all, Katie, I really can't."

She nodded. She was listening. Her eyes were closed and she was trying to see him twelve hours before, to run a film of it in her head.

"Anyway," he continued, "the canoe tipped and I was in the water and I was bumping off rocks, and I thought about the Ellison kid again and I knew—I was sure—I was going to die. The water was coming into my lungs and I was choking, and you know something else? I didn't even mind."

"Aaron!"

"But don't you see? I started to fight it. I grabbed and grabbed until I got hold of that big rock and I stayed there until everything was all right. I fought it, Katie, I fought it! Maybe that's what I had to find out: if I would. And I did."

"And if you hadn't?"

Aaron didn't have any answer for that. His thinking just hadn't gone that far. He shrugged.

"Aaron," she said, softly and evenly now, "you had a lousy thing happen to you and nobody's playing that down, but you just can't solve your problems by running from them, and that's what suicide is, Aaron. It's running."

"I don't think it'll happen again."

"No," she sighed, "I guess I don't either."

"Katie," he said, even more gravely, "there's one more thing."

"Yes, Aaron?"

"Can I get out of here now? Either that or call a plumber."

It was just the release she needed. She laughed until she was gasping and choking. Not a little-girl laugh, but a patented Barlow bellow. Aaron, with his bizarre sense of humor and his penchant for non sequiturs had always been able to do it to her. Like the time he got her going in English class: she was giving an oral book report on *Compulsion* and he slipped a note onto her desk which said, "BOBBY FRANKS WAS A SNOT-TY KID ANYWAY." Later, after their joint deten-tion, he admitted he'd stolen the line from Lenny Bruce.

The laugh became a wicked smile.

"Throw me your clothes."

"What?"

"Your clothes. Throw me your clothes. It's about time you learned how to swim, just in case you do decide to run those rapids again. Come on."

"Promise you won't look?"

"Fat chance."

"Okay, but you'll be sorry." The shoe was the hard-est, what with the laces soaked and the knot simply impossible. Finally he just wrenched it off, and for one second that strange brain of his almost persuaded him that there were some things about being one-legged that were not so bad. He kept that one in. He tossed her the shoe, the sock and, in quick succession, the jeans and the T-shirt. Then, feeling silly for wait-ing, he slipped off the underwear and tossed that too.

Katie spread his clothing over a bush to dry and then, without even a hint of self-consciousness, she stripped off her own T-shirt, jeans and panties—she never wore a bra; never had to, except in competition

—and did a running swan dive, over Aaron and into the deep water behind him.

"Say," Aaron said, "you *have* . . ."

"If you say I've filled out since Brazil, you'll never leave this pond alive. And now, Mark Spitz, the first thing we learn about swimming is to keep our head above water." With that she dunked him.

"Well," he said as he struggled into his stiffening and still-damp clothes, "what do you think: can I make a comeback with the water polo team?"

"The drowning team, maybe . . . But seriously, Aaron, if you could coach, or do something in sports . . ." She was leaning forward, squeezing the water out of her hair, and she didn't see his I-don't-want-to-hear-any-more look. "I mean, you weren't one of the best athletes in the world just because of your body, as wonderful as it is. You worked hard, Aaron, you trained your mind. And what's more, you could talk about what you did, how you did it, you . . ."

"Enough, Katie! Not now, okay? I'll think about it. I promise."

Okay, she thought, there has been enough emotion for one day anyway. She'd take his answer as a qualified maybe, and try later. How like her to try to pack it all in where it couldn't possibly fit. But time *was* running out. Next week she'd be gone and she just had to try to leave Aaron with something to work with. But not now. Tomorrow, maybe.

"Hey, I haven't told you about Brazil."

"I know," he said, "you did great."

"Yeah, but you don't know the best part. You remember how big those East European shot putters are . . ."

"Watch your mouth, girl, you're talking about my ancestors."

"Stop it, Aaron, this is serious." It wasn't, and her face said that. "Anyway, they're getting even bigger. So I'm out there in my well-distributed one hundred and eighteen pounds and they start arriving, and these . . . these female Sumo wrestlers start to arrive. Arms

as big as my thighs. Uniforms stretched over all that
flab. And I'm thinking: how did I let myself get talked
into this, anyway? I mean, I'm not even a shot putter,
it's always been my worst event in the pentathlon, as
you know. But guess what?"

"You beat them?"

"Are you nuts? They beat the hell out of me!"

Laughter. It was nice to feel warm with him again.
And comfortable. Katie, from a very young age, had
insisted on being herself, but with Aaron she didn't
have to insist. What more could a woman ask? Well,
something more, something less definable.

"By the way," Aaron asked, "how did Old Greg do
down there?"

Greg? Does he know? No, it had to be an innocent
question. Then why did she feel her face burning?

"Katie? Something wrong?"

"No, no." Damn, she said it too fast. Slow down
girl. "He did just fine, finished sixth." She almost said,
"you'd have won," but she swallowed the words.
Change the subject. Quick.

"I'm thinking of getting into something different,"
she announced. "Check out a few muscles I haven't
used before. Javelin, maybe. You ever throw the javelin?"

He shook his head. "Tell me, Miz Barlow, is this the
beginning of another one of your pep talks about trying
new things?"

"No, of course not!" She said that too fast as well;
maybe it was. "I'm serious. I really am. Aaron, stop
looking at me like that!"

5

The high school athletic field was almost deserted that Saturday afternoon. The Reverend Tompkins was there, as usual, puffing around the track in his fancy Pony exercise suit, and three laughing boys were taking turns hurling themselves at the long jump pit. The Keller boy, who'd quarterbacked the team to the district championships the previous fall, was practising his drop-back passing at the far end. Aaron, who was sitting in his car, could not see the receiver. Katie had the infield all to herself.

Aaron watched her pick up the javelin, heft it, bring it up to her shoulder, bounce it a couple of times until she gripped precisely at the point of balance, then, for a second or two, stand immobile. Caught up with her action, he breathed with her, and felt the charge beginning in his own muscles. As she started her running approach, his body came slightly out of the seat. As she released he discovered himself surging higher. Aaron didn't know all that much about javelin, but he'd watched the best over the years and he knew one thing: Katie's form was almost perfect; she threw beautifully. Unfortunately, he thought, she also didn't throw very far.

As she trudged back to her starting position, six javelins under her arm, Aaron was out of the car and waiting for her.

"You're late," she said.

"Had a few chores to catch up on," he replied. "Actually," he amended, "I slept in. Best sleep I've had since I've been home."

"Keeps getting better," Katie said, gesturing downfield where a series of little white flags stood.

"What's the red one?" Aaron asked, shielding his eyes from the sun and looking beyond the white markers.

"That's the record," Katie said.

"World?"

"No, Canadian. You see that other red flag?" Aaron had to search. It *was* a long way off. He nodded. "That's the world," Katie said. After a moment of letting the distance sink in, she offered: "You want to try?"

"Thanks," Aaron said, touching his finger to the point of one of the javelins. "I'd probably do myself an injury. I'll just sit instead."

Katie continued to throw, methodically and properly, but still without much distance. After an hour and a half her jersey was soaked with sweat and her throat was raw from all that mouth-breathing and her eyes hurt where the sweat had burned them. She hadn't come close to the Canadian record, much less the world mark that loomed impossibly several yards beyond that.

If Katie was doing this to inspire him, Aaron decided, she wasn't succeeding. She looked downright miserable out there, and the smile she forced her face into was not masking her irritation. It wasn't just that she couldn't fool him with it, she couldn't have fooled a visitor from another planet.

And her irritation was contagious. For Aaron, the first few minutes had been mildly interesting. When that wore off he tried to pretend he was amused, but he soon had to admit to himself that what he really was, was bored. Maybe people—maybe even Katie—had been bored watching him, too, for all those hours he spent running and jumping at that crossbar, but that thought didn't make him feel any more charitable. Besides, his bum was going to sleep.

"Are you going to throw again?" he asked as she

lugged the spears back from yet another unillustrious performance.

"No, I'm going to knit you a sweater," she snapped. "Listen, Aaron, I'm serious about this, so if you don't like it why don't you just bug off."

Which was just about what he wanted to hear. It was beginning to occur to him that it wasn't just having to watch Katie's repetitive rituals that was bothering him anyway. Part of it was just being here, in the place where he'd honed his body for nearly ten years and made it do improbable and wonderful things. And part of it was just being forced to be a spectator.

"You're wasting your time," he muttered. "I'll wait for you in the car." But then he changed his mind and headed off down the field to say hello to Reverend Tompkins, to thank him for the note the minister had sent him while he was in the hospital. Aaron was picking his way through Katie's pattern of flags when he heard the shout.

"Aaron!"

He didn't turn, he didn't even look back. He just dropped there in the dust and the hardened blobs of lime that had been part of last fall's thirty-yard line, waiting for the spear to hit him in the back and pin him to the ground like a butterfly in a biology lab. Instinctively he put his hands back to cover his head. His terror was unfounded; the javelin landed well in front of him, sinking into the hard sun-baked earth just two feet from the red flag that marked the Canadian record.

"See that?" Katie hollered, running up beside him. "See that? Now if I'd listened to *you* I wouldn't even have tried."

Aaron looked at the flag, the javelin and then at Katie. "That . . ." He was going to say, "That was really something," but he recognized the words too well. "Just hand me my crutches, will you," he said gruffly, trying to hide the fact that he was very, very impressed.

Clare and Myles were in bed and nearly asleep when the noises began outside.

"Whatsamatter?" Myles said, startled. He lifted himself a little on one elbow.

"Nothing dear," she said, reassuring him.

"Hmmph," he said, unconvinced. But he lay down again.

"Good, dear." She kissed him between the shoulder blades, pulled up the covers and slipped back into a reverie. For a moment, as she drifted closer and closer to sleep herself, she thought about Aaron and Katie; Katie *did* seem to be getting somewhere with him. She wondered what they were talking about, downstairs in the living room where she and Myles had left them an hour or so before.

Suddenly her eyes snapped wide open. Now *she* had heard the noises.

"What's that?"

"What's what?" Myles grumbled into the pillow.

"Outside. A noise. Listen. See, there it is again." She was already in motion, pulling the flannel housecoat around herself as she rushed to the window. Myles slowly groped after her in the darkness.

"See anything?" He was looking over her shoulder, holding her waist as she leaned farther out, looking left and right for the source of the sound.

"Over there. It's okay, it's Aaron and Katie. They're doing something at Aaron's high jump, that's all."

"At this time of night? What's the matter with them?"

"Myles, it isn't even eleven o'clock yet. Everybody doesn't live the way we do, you know."

"Probably be better off if they did," he grumbled. "I'm going back to bed."

"No, don't. Watch this with me for a while. I think something good is happening down there. Here, snuggle closer. I'll keep you warm." Reluctantly, he complied.

"Maybe," Aaron said, picking dirt and gravel out of his left elbow, "this wasn't such a great idea anyway."

Katie was readjusting the crossbar. "Maybe you're right," she replied, sighing a deep sigh, too deep to be taken seriously. "We've been at this for all those minutes—five, maybe even six—and you still haven't got it."

Okay, he deserved that. Bravely he swung his increasingly-battered body back to the starting line, a two-foot length of three-inch angle iron sunk there by his father a decade ago and now almost overgrown from a year of disuse. What did he want for his thirteenth birthday, his father had asked him. My own high jump, he'd replied without hesitation. On the day of his birthday he'd come home from school and there it was, all finished, the cement not even quite dry under the uprights, the soft, straw-filled burlap sacks that formed the landing area untouched by human back.

"Well," the familiar voice of Katie Barlow broke into his memories, "are you going to try it again or not?"

"Yeah. Sure. I was just remembering something, that's all."

"The way I figure it," she continued, a touch professorily, "what we've got here is a balance problem. Somebody once said 'position is everything' and I always went along with that. But somebody else should have said 'balance is everything'."

"Sounds like somebody just did."

"No, Aaron, I mean it. You get the balance down and everything flows from that. You get what I mean?"

"Right, coach." He was mocking her, but so gently that she didn't even pick up on it. She was tugging at her ear, the way she always did when she was thinking hard. She was dead on though, about the balance.

He stood at his mark, eyed the crossbar and began taking the short, deep breaths that were the first step in the process of clearing his mind, and bringing the whole world into one tight focus at an invisible point a foot or so above the bar. After an extended moment he began his surge forward, oblivious to the pain of the crutches pounding into his armpits.

At the very last demi-second he dropped the right crutch and, using the left like a straight leg, hurled his body up, sideways, approximating as closely as possible his old jumping style.

He hit the bar with his chest and upper arm, carrying it into the pit—a too-thin layer of straw they'd just tossed there for the time being—and landing with his left arm under him. "Shit, Katie, it's no use. Three-and-a-half goddamned feet. I was doing that when I was nine."

"Okay," she said, standing over him and holding his crutches. "You're the one who's taking the beating. Want to call it a night?"

"No, goddamnit," he groaned. "Here, give me the damned crutches."

A fascinated Clare and a grumbling Myles stayed in the window for about fifteen minutes, until he moved away with a grunt of finality and went to the bathroom. She was still watching when he returned, and with some reluctance she managed to tear herself away. Myles was lying on his left side, his back turned toward her—something he only did when he was angry, or upset.

"Myles, is there something wrong?"

"Nothing's wrong."

"It is because Aaron's jumping again? Is that it?"

"Not jumping. Playing. Fooling around."

"Myles . . ."

"NOTHING'S WRONG!" Then, to try to prove the point, he turned over on his back and Clare, seizing the opportunity, snuggled under his arm.

6

Katie didn't see Myles until she was walking back to her towel and sweatsuit, having just run the 100-meter hurdles ten times in succession. He was standing there, holding the towel out to her, an expression on his face that told her he was not at the school athletic field that morning just to pass the time of day, an expression so hostile that it made her stomach go funny.

She took the towel and wiped away the sheen of sweat—the only solid evidence that she'd been exerting herself for more than an hour—and still without speaking, playing his game, climbed into her sweat pants and pulled on the jacket. Myles was walking in little circles, head down. She toyed with the idea of breaking the uncomfortable silence with a comment on the weather, or asking what Myles was doing in town so early in the morning, even inquiring if Aaron was stiff or not after last night's workout.

Katie was accomplished in many things for so young a woman, but she'd never won a silent stand-off in her life. And she suspected, based on some pretty solid first hand knowledge, that Myles Kornylo had never lost one—except to Clare, of course; that went without saying. There was only one reason why he'd be there at that hour of the morning, looking unhappy and wandering around in those infuriating little circles. He'd seen Aaron jumping last night and for some reason he was mad about it. Okay, let's get on with it.

"He was the third best high jumper in the world, Mr. Kornylo. It took a long while to get there, you know. You can't expect him to forget it, just like that."

"He needs to start." He was looking at her now, not directly, but with a kind of three-quarter profile. She could see both of his eyes, and that didn't make her feel any better: they were slits. The first voice she heard in her head told her to shut up and walk away; the second said, stay and fight. Fight him? Fight Mr. Kornylo? Okay, the first voice conceded, if you really have to.

"How do *you* know what he needs?" Even though she'd planned the words, she was still surprised when she heard them. Not as surprised, apparently, as her hulking adversary: his mouth actually fell open. Round one to Barlow, she thought.

"How *could* you know what he needs, Mr. Kornylo. You watched him on the river, in the rapids, and you still can't bring yourself to see what was really happening out there. You still see it as some kind of big, macho adventure, don't you. You can't see . . ."

"He put himself to a test," Myles said, his voice higher and his delivery more rapid than Katie remembered ever having heard it. "And he passed the test. That's what happened on the river. Men do it every day, one way or the other. And don't use those women's libber words like 'ma-cho' on me. Save it for your teen-aged friends."

She opened her mouth to speak, then closed it again. She could feel the hot blood turning her cheeks and ears red and it was small consolation that Myles' face was florid now too. She became aware of the pressure in her chest and exhaled the breath she'd been holding for she-couldn't-remember-how-long.

"Mr. Kornylo," she said in a quiet voice, "what it all comes down to is that he's his father's son. Whatever he does, it'll be his own idea. Nothing you tell him, nothing I tell him, nothing anybody tells him is going to make one damn bit of difference. He decided he wanted to jump again, and he'll decide if he wants to stop."

For just a second there seemed to be acknowledgment in Myles' eyes, a glimmer of understanding. Maybe it had lasted longer than that, but Katie couldn't tell, because all she could see was his back as he walked away.

The sound of the tractor's big engine confused Myles for a moment. He looked at the ancient Roman numeral clock over the kitchen sink and confirmed that it was indeed only 6:20 in the morning. His second piece of toast was in his left hand, his knife in his right, poised over the butter. He looked at Clare, who was sipping her coffee, seemingly oblivious to the sound he was hearing.

"Aaron down already?" he asked.

"About an hour," she replied, sipping again.

His heavy brows came together in a look of puzzlement. Then he allowed himself a flickering smile. He looked up to see if Clare was watching him and, sure enough, she was. Also smiling. Ummph. He hated being caught out that way. His own father wouldn't have been caught dead smiling. Which made him wonder, just for a heartbeat or two, if he'd ever pleased his father, the way Aaron had pleased him so many times—the way Aaron was pleasing him at this very moment. Must have. He just didn't remember, that was all. Enough of this. Time to go to work.

"Morning," Aaron said. "Hand me one of those shims in the box, will you."

Myles fished a couple of washers out of the grease-blackened old toolbox his grandfather had made forty years before, when he was too old to work the land any more and needed something to fill out his days.

"One'll do," Aaron said, taking both.

Myles wandered over to a bale of hay and tugged at the twine. It came off in his hand and the bale began to fall apart. "Still doing that," he muttered.

"Not for much longer, I hope," Aaron replied, prodding at something on the baler that Myles couldn't quite see. What he could see was the intense concentration on his son's face, the tip of the tongue absently licking the lower lip, the eyes fixed on some hidden point down in the machinery. "There," Aaron said at last, handing back the second shim, "that should do it."

But Myles wasn't there to receive the shim. He was over by the tractor, running his hand along the hot engine. It came away with a whitish gunk stuck to his fingers. "You put a new gasket in this tractor?" he asked.

"Yeah," Aaron said, wiping his hands with a kerosene-soaked rag, being very careful not to get any dirt or kerosene into the gash, which was all but healed.

"You getting good pressure out of it?"

"Sure."

"Thought we'd need new valves," Myles said.

"They were scored a bit," Aaron said, coming around to stand beside his father. "But I ground them good as new." This, he began to realize, was a nice conversation; he hoped he could find a way to keep it going.

"You're the one always talking about people buying new things instead of fixing the old ones . . . these bearings are pretty worn, though: I think I've got my work cut out for me."

Myles walked over and peered into the inner workings of the binder. What he saw pleased him, though he didn't let on.

"How would you like your bales tied?" Aaron persevered. "Maybe we can get it to make a fancy bow. The cows will think it's Christmas."

"Simple hitch is fine," Myles allowed. He was smiling again. It was okay, though, because nobody could see it. The only one around was Aaron, and he was head-first into the machinery.

"Looks in line," Aaron announced, finally. "Shouldn't have any trouble with the bales now." He slid the metal hatchcover into place and bolted it down. "Okay," he said. "All set."

"Let's start her up then," Myles said. "See if we're in business here." For the first time in weeks, no, *months,* he was allowing himself to feel good. Aaron

seemed so . . . what? Content. Yes, content. This was
the son that Myles had expected, had been waiting for,
a true heir. Myles congratulated himself. He'd been
right all along. But he wouldn't say it, now or ever.
He'd just let it happen and enjoy it.

He climbed up into the tractor, which started at his
touch. He shoved in the clutch pedal, engaged the
baler and, after two rotations of the drive arm, a perfect bale of hay landed in front of Aaron. He fingered
the twine, then, looking very self-satisfied, gave his
father the thumbs-up salute. Myles switched off the
tractor and dropped easily to the ground. "She's all
yours, son," he said, almost beaming, no longer trying
to disguise the fact.

"Dad," Aaron began, "I have to shower. Katie's
picking me up. She's got some place for us to go. A
surprise, she . . ." He didn't finish because he suddenly realized that the smile on his father's face was
gone. The eyes were narrowed, colder. The short truce
was broken. He'd broken it. Desperately, and not too
effectively, he tried to backtrack, to make up.

"I'll start in early tomorrow, dad. Hay's still a little
wet anyway. Do you mind?"

Myles was back up in the tractor. "You got something to do," he said frostily, "you go and do it."
Aaron watched the line of perfect bales trail out behind the baler as his father drove off into the sun.

"Shit," he said.

7

"Okay," Katie said as they passed the sign that said Welcome To Willow Creek and listed the service clubs, "are you going to tell me or not?"

"Tell you what?" Aaron asked back.

"You know. Why you wore your prosthesis this morning."

"A surprise. You said you had a surprise for me, so I found one for you."

"Ohh-kay . . ."

The fact is, he wasn't sure why himself. He'd sat on the bed after his shower looking at the damn thing, and just decided that maybe it wasn't such a damn thing after all. That was about it. So he spent a few minutes digging out the pieces of glass left over from his Night of the Long Wooden Legs, reviewed the physiotherapist's instructions, and just strapped it on. It still didn't feel all that great, but it didn't feel all that bad either.

Katie drove the Chevy into the high school parking lot, brought it in beside an equally-battered, equally-old Plymouth, and killed the engine.

"Why are we here today?" Aaron asked. "You work out on alternate days, don't you? Besides, watching you work out—no offence—is not my idea of a great surprise."

"Come on, you'll see."

55

Partway across the parking lot, Aaron started falling behind.

"Is it okay?" Katie asked, slowing down enough that he caught up with her.

"Still hurts a little," Aaron replied, rubbing at the point where the prosthesis attached to his stump. "I feel like what's-his-name . . . you know . . . Chester."

"The cane doesn't help?"

"Maybe when I get used to it. Say, I really do want to know what we're doing here. I don't hop another step until you tell me what this is all about."

She pointed to a group of people standing around the high jump apparatus at the far end of the field. All save one were in white T-shirts and light-blue shorts. They seemed to be listening intently to the larger, older figure, who was in a blue track suit, and who had a whistle hung around his neck.

"That's Jim Rainfeld," Katie said. "You know: he came in the spring, when Mr. Beatty had the heart attack. I met him the other day when I was working out here and we talked for a while and your name came up and . . . Well, anyway, he's going to let you take over today's session."

"Hey!" Aaron stopped. "Hey! Now just a damn minute!"

Katie took his arm, sternly, like a mother leading her balky son to the Saturday night bathtub. "Come on, Aaron. The best way to see how you feel about coaching is to try it, right?"

"Wrong," Aaron corrected, trying to pull away from her. "You had no right to lay this on me. Come on, let's get out of here."

"Aaron?" She sounded genuinely surprised. "I thought you wanted to coach. You said you wanted to coach."

"No," he corrected again, "you said I *should* coach. I didn't say anything. That's not the same thing, Katie, not the same thing at all."

"But . . ." It was too late. Rainfeld was almost upon them, within hearing distance and closing rapidly. They both shut up.

"Hi, Katie," Rainfeld said, reaching out his hand to shake hers. God, Aaron thought, one of those compulsive hand-shakers. Wonder if he'll slap her on the back, too? But when the man turned to him, Aaron shifted the cane to his left hand and accepted Rainfeld's too-hardy clasp. "Aaron!" Rainfeld said enthusiastically. "It's a pleasure. I've seen you jump. Matter of fact I was in Montreal when you won the bronze. I probably cheered as loud as anybody."

"Yeah," Aaron said.

If disinterest had been a disease, Aaron observed, Rainfeld would have had an epidemic on his hands. "Men," Rainfeld announced to the seven sullen boys, "for those of you who don't know him, this is Aaron Kornylo, the best . . ." He glanced down at Aaron's leg and at the cane. ". . . his Canadian record still hasn't been broken. And you all know he won the bronze medal in the Olympics." He checked Aaron's face, apparently to see if he was doing all right. Aaron just stared straight ahead, feeling the blood rising hot in his cheeks. He was going to say something—something not nice—but Katie sensed it and squeezed his bicep. Hard. He let his eyes wander over the faces of the students. The singular lack of enthusiasm they showed was matched only by the singular lack of enthusiasm he felt. Nevertheless, for Katie's sake he'd somehow try to get through this embarrassment.

"Well," he said, "talking about high jumping isn't going to help anyone. You've got to do it."

"Right!" shouted Rainfeld. "Let's go!"

"Right!" Aaron mimicked, under his breath. "Let's go!"

The first kid—Weiller, his name was—cleared the four-foot bar with an adequately executed western roll. He came up nonchalantly and trotted back to the others. But when he thought nobody was looking, he searched Aaron's face for approval. There was none.

"You all see that?" Aaron asked, looking from face to expressionless face. "What he just did? Well, forget it, 'cause he did it wrong. It's not the right style." He didn't see Weiller's face fall. He didn't see Rainfeld squirm. He didn't see Katie wince. What he did see was two boys standing a little back from the other, whispering.

"You say something?" he challenged the taller one.

"Langely," Rainfeld said, pointing his finger. "Shut up and listen!"

"If you're really serious about jumping—and it's not worth doing unless you are—you have to use the back-layout technique," Aaron continued, thinking of Katie and trying to act like he thought a coach should act. "That's the Olympic style . . . All right, I want a volunteer." After a pause for the response, which did not come, Aaron tried to make a joke. "It's okay," he said. "It's not a kamikaze mission." Nobody laughed. Well screw them.

"Ohh-kay. Hey, you in the back. What's your name? Langely, is it?"

"Langely!" the coach shouted.

"Right," said Aaron. "That's my man. Langely, why don't you come up here and see what you can do."

Katie was beside him now, hissing in his ear.

"Take it easy, Aaron. Remember, they're just kids."

"Kids, eh?" He put as much malice into those two words as he could muster. Let her squirm, let her stand there and try to figure out how she's going to explain this to her pal Rainfeld later. He was rolling. "Anyway," he told her, "this isn't for their benefit, it's for mine. Remember?" He broke the last word into syllables.

"Now, Langely . . ." He found himself looking into a bobbing Adam's apple. He started again, this time looking the kid directly in the eye. "Now, Langely, can you jump that?"

"Sure."

"Good. Mr. Rainfeld, let's have it up to five." When that was accomplished he took Langely aside and explained: "Okay, now you're going to do a back layout over it. You go off on your left leg, throw your right leg over and arch your back. You got that?"

"Yeah," Langely said, doing his best to sound

bored but feeling a cold little ball developing in his stomach. "Yeah, I got it."

"So let's see it."

Rainfeld had a worried look on his face, the look of a man with visions of an angry principal and angry parents in his office, demanding an explanation for a student's broken arm. "Maybe," he whispered to Katie, "we should lay down some sawdust or something first. That sand looks awful hard for a landing from that height."

But Aaron overheard. "Langely's not worried about his landing," he sneered. "Langely's not even worried about getting over the bar—*are* you, Langely? Are you ready, Langely?"

The ball in his stomach was getting bigger and wetter, and his Adam's apple was bouncing up and down. His throat was too dry for him to chance talking, so he just nodded.

There was nothing wrong with Langely's take-off, but in mid-flight old habits and new pressures took over. He brought his legs up into a tuck and his shoulders hit the bar, which he carried partway with him on the way to the hard ground. His back hit first and there was an audible "whoosh" as the air was driven from his lungs. As he lay there, fighting for breath, he looked up to see Aaron's unsympathetic face. He also saw the helping hand that Rainfeld had proffered, and shook it off. After about thirty seconds he slowly rose to the sitting position; in another thirty seconds he was back, not-too-steadily, on his feet.

"I'm okay," he confirmed.

"Drop it back to four feet and go back to the western roll," Rainfeld said, studiously ignoring both Aaron and Katie.

"I'm sorry, Jim," Katie said.

"Sure." When he turned to Aaron he was no longer the hand-shaking, back-slapping jock. "They still have a lot to learn about technique," he said evenly, "but so do you. If you can ever manage to get that chip off your shoulder, come and see us again." Then he turned, dismissing both.

Katie said nothing all the way to the car. She said
nothing most of the way back to the farm. Aaron also
kept the peace. They were going to have one hell of a
fight—he knew that—but he was not going to be the
one to start it. He wasn't feeling all that good about
Katie, right at that moment, and he knew the feeling
was mutual.

Finally she said: "If it had been me I would have
punched you."

"Bad move," he responded, without a trace of humor. "They arrest people for beating up on a cripple."

She bit her lip. She was going to swear, but she
was just too angry. "You're a prize, you know that?"
she spluttered. "A real *prize!*" Then: "I really did
think you wanted to coach. You did let me think that,
Aaron, you did!"

"Watch where you're going," he said as the car
swung dangerously close to the ditch on his side, "I'm
down to three limbs already."

When the car was back in its lane and moving ap-
preciably slower, he answered her question.

"No, I don't want to coach. I would have told you
that earlier if I'd known where you were taking me.
That whole damn fiasco is as much your fault as mine.
More. You're mad at me because I didn't live up to
your expectations. Well, I'm mad at you, too. You're
pushing me too hard, Katie, you're pressuring too
much." No, that was too harsh, too unfair. He owed
her more than that. "I have to have my own expectations, Katie, and right now coaching isn't one of
them."

It had a sobering effect. "Why?" she asked, "why
not coaching?"

"Because it's not enough." He was explaining now,
rather than accusing. "Those kids don't want to learn,
they're just out to have fun."

"And what's wrong with high jumping being fun?"
He didn't bother to remind her that it wasn't that much
fun for her; in the pentathlon it was her next-to-worst
event, right behind shotput.

"Nothing," he said. "But it's no good for us . . . for me, anyway." He turned on the seat to talk to her profile, to try to make her understand; he was having trouble figuring out why she didn't already understand, why she didn't *know*. Or, to be fair, maybe he hadn't known before either, about how much it truly meant. Maybe, he thought, you have to lose it before you can really appreciate it for the incredible thing that it is.

"Jumping was the main part of my life. It may not have been everything, but it was almost everything. It was the one thing that was unlimited, open-ended. Each time I'd jump a little higher and I felt . . . I felt like I was defying gravity, that I was doing something *impossible*. Remember how I couldn't make seven feet for a long time, how I thought that was my limit? Then I did. Do you remember that day? After that I knew there was no limit, that I could just keep going higher and higher . . ."

"Okay," she said as the car came to rest in the farm yard, "what do you want to do?"

Did he dare tell her? What if she laughed? Worse, what if she thought he was crazy? At this point he wasn't even sure if he could defend himself, or the idea that had only come into his head less than forty-eight hours before as he lurched repeatedly at that crossbar in the dark of the farmyard. But she *did* ask.

"Jump," he said, almost bouncing out of the car so he wouldn't have to see the look on her face. "I want to jump," he repeated, slamming the door. "I want to compete!" he shouted as he half-bounded across the yard.

Katie thought about it all the way home. And the more she thought about it the less crazy the idea sounded. After all, some—most—of the athletes in the Disabled Games were doing phenomenal things. Who was that one-armed discus thrower who was getting distances almost equal to Olympics—regular Olympics—qualification standards? There were others too, she knew, who could do unbelievable things despite loss of limbs, partial paralysis, and even blindness. And Aaron? Aaron still had his athlete's mind and training and desire; he was in pretty good condition. Technique was a problem, of course: she'd have to start thinking about technique.

8

Aaron was already in a happy sweat when Katie arrived, late the following afternoon. He'd been doing calisthenics for nearly forty minutes and his body felt hard, flexible and responsive.

"Good news," she greeted him. "I called George Hayman after I left you yesterday and he promised to put applications for the Disabled Games in the mail. They're next month, you know, in Edmonton."

"Uh-uh," Aaron shook his head. "I want the Olympic trials."

Katie started walking in little circles, throwing her hands in the air. "Aaron, Aaron! For godsake I thought you were going to be realistic!" Then she stopped, faced him and spoke almost as parent to child. "First, you don't have enough power in your leg. Second, I doubt if they'd let you compete even if you could."

He simply ignored her. He limped over, set the crossbar up six inches to five feet, unstrapped his prosthesis, pinned up the leg of his sweatpants, and climbed on the crutches. He stood on his starting mark, talking to himself, but loudly enough so that Katie could overhear.

"You know . . . I look at that bar and I tell myself there's just no reason why I can't. I'm still the same person. I mean mentally I can still jump seven feet, six inches. It's just that physically, I have this little problem." He stopped talking and thought for a moment. "Technique . . . I'll have to change my technique . . . but I know I'm going to be able to do it."

For a long moment he stood there, psyching himself, then he swung off the mark, gathering momentum. This time he let go of one crutch and planted the other in front of himself at the very last second, attempting to vault over the bar. It wasn't even close. As he picked himself up he looked over at Katie who seemed for all the world like she was stifling a laugh. So, he suddenly realized, was he.

"I wonder," he said, scrunching up his brow in mock-seriousness, "if they'll let me pole vault over with a crutch?"

They had their laugh. Then Katie became very stern and ever-so-practical again. "Aaron, come on. This is good exercise for you, but that's all it is."

"Hmmph," he replied, replacing the crossbar, gathering up his crutches and going back to the starting mark. This time he hit the left upright, taking it into the foam mats along with himself and the crossbar.

"Seems I have to work on the takeoff," he said, his good humor undiminished.

"A straight dive . . ." Katie murmured.

"What's that?" Aaron asked.

"Nothing."

"No. You said: 'straight dive.' That's not legal, though."

"Actually," she said, "it is—if you only take off on one foot."

"In my case," he laughed, getting up, "there's not a lot of choice."

His body cleared the bar easily. The crutch didn't.

"Got to figure a way of dumping the crutches," he said. After five more attempts, all failures, Katie thought she had the answer. "No crutch," she said. "Forget the crutches."

"Right," he said. "No crutch . . . No *crutch?*"

Following her advice, he let go of the crutches just before starting his next jump. In the part of a second that left him on one leg, there was no time to lose his balance. He sprang and dived and even before he was over the bar, even without being able to see the distance between it and him, he knew he'd topped it by at least six inches. Oh, Christ, what a wonderful feeling, the chills starting at the small of his back and running all the way up into his scalp, the warm ball in his belly, the . . .

"Great," Katie said with less enthusiasm than he'd expected, "but you were lucky. The crutches might just as easily have hit the upright as not. No, we'll have to go one step further, do the whole thing without them. Can you?"

There was only one way to find out, Aaron decided, and that was to try it. Leaving his crutches at the starting mark, he began hopping forward on his one leg, like a man on a pogo stick. Halfway he toppled over. Katie helped him up and supported him back to the starting position. "This," he gasped, "will take some getting used to."

The third time he actually got to his takeoff point, but as he sprang he went off to the right, hitting the upright with his shoulder. "Thinking too much about falling," he grunted. "That's all. Throwing me off."

Each time he tried—and failed—he made new adjustments. By the ninth attempt his hopping approach had become almost smooth and fluid; he concentrated more and more on the takeoff now, getting that extra power; and the dive was taking care of itself, a natural result of all that had gone before it. As his body hit, back first, he executed a flip and looked happily at Katie. Then, partly in self-mockery, partly in self-pride, he slowly raised his arms in victory.

"By George," Katie said, badly faking an English accent, "I think he's got it!"

"By George," Aaron replied, "I think he does!"

Whatever was happening, Myles was beginning to like it. For nearly two weeks now, ever since Aaron had started that one-legged high jumping, he'd been like a different person. He never sulked, he never complained, he did things without being asked. Like that very morning: Myles was still brushing his teeth when he heard the tractor start up and head off to the north. It was only eight-thirty or so when it returned, the haybaler behind it, a smiling Aaron at the controls.

"She's running like a sweetheart," Aaron announced, hopping down and walking over to his father. The limp, Myles noticed, was pronouncedly diminished: Aaron wore the prosthesis all the time now, except when he was jumping and, of course, when he was sleeping. He had also started calling people "Misstur Dillon," which had to be explained to Katie, who had never seen the early *Gunsmoke,* not even in reruns (where Aaron picked it up) but not to Myles and Clare: it had been Myles' favorite program.

"Just a sweetheart," Aaron repeated as he closed in on his father. "Almost done with the back sixty."

Myles looked up from the fertilizer spreader, which he'd been scraping. He considered the cloudless sky for a moment. He picked up a handful of dirt and let it sift through his fingers. He scanned his fields.

"We get more rain," he finally said, "and we should get another two hayings off it before snow. Wheat could use it too." Neither man realized it, but Myles, in his strange way, was running a test. He'd been watching, and he'd been guessing, but, whether he'd ever admit it or not, he wanted to hear it. And he did.

"Wouldn't count on rain," Aaron replied, "but you never know." He suddenly realized what he had just said. It sounded just like something his father would say, and just the way he would say it. It was something a farmer would say. He looked over at Myles to see if he had picked up this . . . this, uhh . . . what was it, an admission of guilt? What did he expect, that his father would reach over with that big hard hand and grab him by the arm and yell "Gotcha?" Someday, Aaron promised himself, he'd learn to read that man's face.

"Treat the land fair, it'll treat you fair back," was all Myles said. This time Aaron smiled, right at him, and Myles could resist no longer: he smiled back.

"You really love this old farm, don't you?" Aaron said, moving to stand beside his father, almost but not quite touching, so they could look out over the land together and see the same things at the same time. Myles, embarrassed, hating to be accused of any show of sentimentality, fumbled for an answer.

"How can you love something that doesn't love you back?" was the best he could come up with.

"What makes you think it doesn't?" Aaron grinned. It had taken twenty three years, but he was finally beginning to understand his father's ways. When he was seventeen, Aaron, like most children, had reached the conclusion that his parents were dumb, hopeless, incapable of change and of understanding. Wasn't it amazing, he said to himself with a self-deprecating grin, how much they'd learned in the last six years?

"Get out of here," Myles ordered, throwing a playful backhander at his son. "Talking nonsense . . ."

"Whatever you say, Misstur Dillon," Aaron said, exaggerating his limp as he headed toward the house.

Clare stood over the sink, absently peeling the potatoes. After a lifetime on the job, she didn't have to look as she whizzed off the brown skins and dropped the spuds into the pot of salted water to her left. Thus freed, she was able to watch Aaron, out in the yard, hopping short sprints on one leg, the calf and ankle now encased in fifteen pounds of buckshot weights.

"Too bad there's no Olympics hopscotch competition, she said to Katie, who was sitting cross-legged on the floor behind her, shucking corn. "He'd win hands down."

"Reminds me," Katie replied, breaking off the small end of a cob, where the niblets were shrunken and unappetizing. "Have to send a letter to the Olympics committee soon. Tomorrow."

Clare had been meaning to talk to her about all

this, and maybe now was as good a time as any. She put down the peeler, wiped her hands on her apron, and was just in the process of turning to Katie when the phone rang. One long, two short. She waited. It repeated. Yes, the call was for them.

"Hello . . . yes, yes she's here." Clare put her hand over the mouthpiece. "For you," she said to Katie. "Long distance." Katie was puzzled. Who could be calling her here, long distance?

"Yes?" she answered tentatively. Then her voice warmed. "Oh, hi Greg."

Clare Kornylo prided herself on being a practical woman, a realist. Which, considering the fact that she was married to a man who fought reality on an average of twice a week, and mother to his father's son, was just as well. But for seventeen days she'd been more than moderately successful in blocking Greg Dubois and what he meant to Katie—to all of them —from her mind. Katie hadn't mentioned it, and neither had she. Maybe, she'd decided, after a week had passed and Katie was still around, it really wasn't going to happen, Katie would not take off and leave Aaron. Then, after two weeks . . . Welcome back to the real world, Clare Kornylo.

Katie turned her back to Clare and spoke softly. All Clare could hear was the odd word, the rest was a muffled whisper. She didn't mean to eavesdrop—or maybe she did, because rather than leaving the room she returned to her potatoes at the sink, and to watching her son out in the yard. She deliberately made little noises—dropping the peeler, turning the taps on and off, crinkling the bag she was dropping the peelings into —trying to convey to Katie's back that she really wasn't interested in what was being said.

Katie's voice became more audible, indicating nothing more than that the conversation was ending.

"Yes, I know. I said I was sorry. I really am . . . yes I do . . . No, I can't. Listen, I'll call you tomorrow, okay? Yeah . . . yeah, you too! I really have to go. Bye."

The two women did not look at one another. Each felt slightly awkward. With every tick of the noisy old clock the silence grew more and more uneasy. Clare continued to peel, Katie continued to shuck.

Katie was no match for Clare, whose twenty-five years married to Myles Kornylo had prepared her well for silent standoffs. "You pick up that track shoe in town?" she asked, a little too brightly.

"Looks good," Clare nodded.

"Great! Did they do what I said? Did they match my design?"

Clare nodded again.

"Great," Katie repeated, her voice too high-pitched, too full of enthusiasm, too nothing's-wrong-honest. "Let's give it to him at dinner."

"No," Clare said quickly. Then, more slowly: "I'll give it to him . . . later." She wasn't too pleased with the way her words were coming out either.

"What . . ." Katie began, hurt and puzzled. Then she stopped and looked away. "Sure," she amended. "Whatever you want . . . Only . . ."

"Only *what?*" Clare snapped. To hell with it, let's get it out and get it over with. "He still doesn't know you're going off to Montreal with that Greg fellow, does he?"

"Greg Dubois," Katie replied. She was trying not to sound defensive, and the result was she sounded a little foolish. "You remember. I . . ."

"Aaron doesn't know, does he?"

"No." She stood up and walked around the room, picking up a Peg Bracken cookbook and examining it like she'd never seen it, or anything like it, before.

Clare sat down at the table. Impatiently she pushed back the tendrils of hair that fell over her forehead. She wasn't being dramatic, just searching for the right words. At last they came.

"You've helped him get a lot stronger, Katie, but not that strong. Not yet. When you tell him, he's going to need someone."

"Clare? I . . . uhh . . . I didn't know you were so . . . so angry with me"

"I'm not." Which was true. If she had been a few minutes before, she wasn't now. "And I'm not looking to take away from anything you've done. I'm just practical . . . I'm just being practical. What he's doing out there right now, that's you. Not Myles. Not me. *You*. He thinks about you different from the way he thinks about us . . . but you know that."

"Clare . . ."

"If he's going to be hurt—if he's got to be hurt—let it happen quickly, so he can get on with the business of living." She reached over and lifted Katie's chin with her hand, looked her directly in the eyes, then took her hand away. "You've always been honest with him, Katie," she said softly. "And I love you for that . . . So does he."

She let the words and the expression on her face sink in. Then she added, even more softly: "Don't stop now."

Katie stood up and came around the table. Clare was also standing. They reached out for one another, and Clare pulled Katie, who was now crying, into her arms. Through her tears Katie caught a glimpse of Aaron out in the yard, doing chin-ups. There was a big dumb happy smile on his face. It was infectious.

"I'll give him the shoe," she said.

Aaron studied the perfectly-wrapped package that had been placed on the table before him. Tentatively he started to untie the bow, but then a lifetime of tearing open Christmas and birthday presents took charge, and he eagerly shredded the paper to get at whatever was inside. "It's a shoe!" To the untrained eye it was no different from any other shoes he'd worn in competition—red suede, white leather and rubber, tri-striped—but Aaron could see the modifications, the increased thickness under the ball of the foot, the slight curl-down of the toe, the abbreviated spikes. "Wait right here," he told everybody.

Ten minutes later he was back, sweaty, a little dusty,

and beaming from ear to ear. "This is incredible," he announced. "Who figured out the design?"

"Beats me," said Clare.

"Me too," said Myles.

"Some genius," said Katie.

9

"You've got an audience," Katie informed him as he set up the high-jump apparatus in the school yard. The equipment and the pit were no better than he had at home; he had just wanted a change of scene. Besides, it gave him an approximation of jumping in a stadium, of what it felt like.

For a moment Aaron didn't recognize the tall boy leaning against the fence.

"He's the one you had your jollies with, isn't he?" Katie asked. "The one I thought should have punched you? Langely, isn't it?"

"Yeah," Aaron laughed. "I guess I didn't scare him off . . . Jesus, he *is* big, isn't he?"

"Do you want to wait a while? Till he goes, I mean?"

"Nope," Aaron said. Instead he gestured at the boy to come over. "Langely! Hey, Langely! Come join us."

"Anybody want to see a one-legged high jumper get a bloody nose?" Katie asked a non-existent audience.

"Oh, ye of little faith," Aaron replied.

Langely sauntered toward them, looking far more apprehensive than combative. He had heard about the athletic exploits of Aaron Kornylo and Katie Barlow for nearly half of his young life, and even seeing Aaron at his worst, a few weeks before, hadn't totally demolished the myth. There was still a fair amount of awe left, but the unwritten code of contemporary teenage behavior prevented him now, as it had before, from showing it.

"How are you doing?" Aaron asked affably.

"Fine. Well, okay," Langely answered.

"How's the form?"

"Working on it." He hadn't been, but that was something he couldn't admit. Not here. Not now.

"Want to try one?" Aaron asked.

"Your way?" Langely withdrew perceptibly.

"Hey, it's not just mine. It's the way somebody figured out you get the best lift. You almost had it the other time, you know. You just stiffened the outside leg too soon. You sure you don't want to try one?"

"Sure."

"Sure you do? Or sure you don't?"

"Sure I do."

"Anyway," Aaron said, "you'll notice I've got the mats out this time. Here, give me a hand arranging them."

Aaron reached up and put his arm on Langely's shoulder, steering him back to the starting position. "Listen Langely . . . uh, what's your first name?"

"Barry."

"Mine's Aaron . . . Listen, Barry, I'm sorry about your landing the last time. It was my fault. I was taking something out on you that I had no right to do." Langely looked at Aaron in a very new way. "This time it'll be no sweat," Aaron said. "I promise."

Aaron left Langely at the starting position and joined Katie at the uprights.

"You didn't have to say all that," she whispered.

"I know," Aaron whispered back. "Maybe that's why it came so easy." He turned to Langely.

"Okay," he instructed, "now think out every move you're going to make from right there. Lock your mind into your muscles. When you're ready, when you feel you're ready, take off."

Langely cleared the five-foot high bar with plenty of daylight. He landed easily. He laughed, mostly with astonishment. "Hey!"

"Good jump!" Katie cheered.

"You got it, fella," Aaron said. "Now all you have to do is make it bigger."

Langely could only repeat: "Hey!"

Leaving Langely to bask a little longer, Aaron went to the left upright and began fiddling with the clamp that held the crossbar. "Katie?" he motioned.

"What are you going to do?" she asked, moving to the other upright.

"You've got to hit six-eight to qualify, don't you?" he said, as the bar was raised nine inches above his head. Langely was on his feet now, using his height to help Katie finish adjusting her side. When he heard what Aaron had said, and realized he wasn't kidding, Langely's mouth dropped open.

"You going to jump six-eight?"

"I'm sure as hell going to try," Aaron replied, sitting on the sparse burnt grass, hauling off the sweatsuit he wore over shorts and a tank-top, and unstrapping his leg.

"Try?" Katie feigned admonishment. "Try? O *who* of little faith? Do it, Kornylo!"

As impatient as he was, Aaron still spent his customary fifteen minutes limbering up, stretching, and pogo-sticking on his left leg. Without so much as a break or a word he went to his starting position, brought mind and body into one focus, and began his approach.

Katie's body involuntarily tensed as her mind ran with Aaron's. So did Langely's. Neither breathed.

The crossbar came closer, closer. Aaron felt the power surging through his leg, down, down to the ends of the toes. He was elated, almost euphoric, light enough to just sail over that bar. He planted the toes, he dived. Up! Higher! Turn! Tuck!

Aaron looked up at the crossbar. He raised his arms in victory. He was laughing. He heard the applause —from a huge, almost-disbelieving crowd of two. Katie was suddenly in the pit with him, her arms around him, kissing him, half-laughing and half-crying. "Fantastic! Oh, Aaron! Fantastic!" Then Langely arrived with the prosthesis and the sweat suit. The look on his face suggested he had just witnessed a miracle. "Way to go!" he kept repeating, "Way to go!"

"Want to try it again?" Katie asked, extricating herself.

"Naahh," Aaron drawled from the side of his mouth. "You've done one, you've done 'em all."

As they walked toward the car, Langely called to them. He was still standing by the apparatus. "Hey . . ." he said. "Thanks. Thanks a lot."

With Katie at the wheel, Saskatoon was just over an hour away. Fifteen minutes after that they were in front of George Hayman's desk.

"Six feet, eight inches?" he asked.

Katie and Aaron both nodded. Then, just in case Hayman hadn't been looking, Aaron said: "Uh-huh." He pushed a file folder across the desk. "Here are my training papers . . . I want to go to Toronto for the trials this week."

Hayman considered what he had in front of him. He reconsidered it. To give himself more time he took off his glasses and rubbed thoughtfully at the reddish depressions the nosepieces had left.

"You've applied to the committee?" he finally asked. Part of him hoped that he would have nothing more to do with this than a handshake and a wish of "good luck."

"I was hoping you'd enter me," Aaron said.

"What about a coach?" That same part of him was still looking for some way out.

"I'm his coach." Katie spoke softly. It was the first time it had occurred to her that she was indeed a coach, had been for the past month or so. It hit her almost as a joke: everything she'd ever learned about high jumping, she'd learned from Aaron. Everything! In her mind, she was—had been—just a good friend, helping out. But, she thought to herself, if it comes down to titles I guess I *am* his coach.

His reluctance now fully conquered, Hayman straightened up Aaron's papers, put them back in the folder, and said: "Well, I'll certainly qualify you,

Aaron. The only trouble now is that you'll both need funding and all of our money's been allocated. The Olympic committee will pick up the hotel and the meals, as you know, but you've got to get there and back. About two hundred dollars, maybe."

"I've got enough put aside for my fare and expenses," Katie said, "and enough for my own trials in Vancouver next month."

"I'll get my share somehow," Aaron promised.

Katie had one last, very important, question.

"George . . . do you think the committee will approve?"

If he'd had doubts previously, he didn't have them at this very moment. He too was caught up in the excitement, the bizarreness of what was happening.

"We're cutting it close," he said, "but I'll get the application on a plane this afternoon. I'll use a courier service. The executive committee will have it first thing tomorrow. That's the last day of their meeting. That's what I mean by cutting it close." He paused, had one negative thought for a fleeting moment, then dismissed it.

"But if you're jumping six feet, eight inches, they can't say no." He reached out his hand to Aaron. He said, "Good luck," then, "you . . . you really think you can do it?"

"I wouldn't be here if I didn't."

"Well, I suppose, just for the record, I'd better see it," he said.

"Hey," Katie said, reaching across the car seat to jostle Aaron's knee, "wake up. I'm getting bored and I want some nice lively conversation."

"Wasn't asleep," Aaron replied. Which was true. Almost asleep, but not quite.

"Great imitation," Katie said, swerving the car around a pothole that the highway crews of spring had either missed or neglected.

"I was just thinking . . ."

"So? A penny . . ."

He slid a little farther down the seat, as far as he

could until the belt stopped him. He held his hands in front of his eyes and examined them, back and front. He rubbed them together. Finally he decided there was no harm in saying it.

"Has it ever occurred to you that this whole thing is just a little bit crazy?"

"Oh, Aaron, it is *not*."

"It isn't?"

"Hell no . . . It's a *lot* crazy."

"But I love it," he laughed.

"Me too," she laughed back.

10

Myles paced the kitchen, stopping every couple of turns to peer out through the screen door. It was one of his assortment of ways of telling Clare that he was upset, that he was giving her her cue to question him, to find out why. Sometimes it worked, sometimes it didn't. This time it didn't.

"Wonder where they are today?" He tried to make it sound like an innocent question, but Myles Kornylo was about as capable of asking innocent questions as he was of laughing at his own foibles, which was to say, not at all.

But something was up. He had this feeling and he was looking for supporting evidence. For nearly a month, Aaron had been just about everything he thought he wanted in a son, and Myles had to admit that the high jumping must be related. Still, when they finished up each day's work and Aaron put on his shorts and went out to the apparatus with Katie, Myles felt uncomfortable. Every evening he was uncomfortable. But then, the next morning, as he and Aaron cheerfully went off together to work the fields, Myles was able to tell himself that he was probably just imagining things, that he was being unfair.

Today was different, though, because Aaron hadn't been there that morning to allay Myles' discomfort. What's more, he hadn't said where he was going. Yes, something was definitely up and Myles didn't like it one damn bit.

"Sorry, Myles," Clare looked up from her turnips, which were just beginning to turn soft in the boiling water. "I didn't hear you." She had, of course.

"Nothing," he muttered, taking up another short vigil at the screen door. "Just wondered where Aaron was, that's all." Since their short but angry battle in the school grounds, Myles had made a point of not mentioning Katie's name. It was not that he could ignore her existence—she was there almost every day, after all—and he did manage to be polite. And it was not even that he was angry with her for what she'd said to him, because down deep he knew that she was right, at least about Aaron if not about him. She couldn't know what he'd felt, standing on that river bank, watching his only son almost die. And he couldn't tell her.

"I think they went to Saskatoon," Clare said finally.

"What for?"

"I don't know."

How come she always knew what he was thinking, and he never knew what she was thinking, Myles wondered. Far off, just below the horizon, he spotted a tiny moving dust-cloud, meaning that within a few minutes Aaron would be home.

"Just in time for supper," he said.

"Pardon?"

He pointed. "There they are."

Though Aaron and Katie and Myles and Clare were in the same room, at the same table, eating the same food, they were not dining together.

For the first twenty minutes, the meal was eaten in a silence broken only by the occasional scrape of knife on plate, the chomp of teeth breaking into fresh buttered corn, and formal requests for foods and seasonings. In his head Aaron was anticipating the conversation that must ultimately come, and dreading it not a little. He "wrote" his openers. He rewrote. He

tried to frame answers for questions his father would
ask, rebuttals for arguments he would make. Katie was
doing much the same thing, though she hoped her supporting role would not be required. While Clare had
correctly guessed the outcome of their trip to Saskatoon, she still had not been officially informed; she
was ready to back her son against her husband—if it
came to that—but she was not rehearsing. Myles just
ate and scowled.

Aaron placed his knife and fork ever-so-correctly
on his plate, and dabbed his lips and chin with his
napkin. He started to clear his throat, then decided,
on second thought, that the placement of the knife and
fork wasn't ever-so-correct enough; he shifted them to
the right side of the plate. He also decided that the second half of his sourdough roll, which he hadn't wanted
moments before, looked kind of good after all. When
he finished that, he took a sip of water. Then another
sip. Finally, in an act that was more of desperation
than bravery, he coughed. Katie and Clare looked up.
Myles didn't.

"Dad?"

Myles nodded. That was all.

"Dad, my jumping is coming along very well."

Another nod.

Well, Aaron, nobody said it was going to be easy.
He stumbled on, aware now that Katie and his mother
had stopped eating too and were watching him intently. Katie, in fact, still had her knife and fork in
her hands.

"I mean really well, dad. I . . ."

"Good exercise," Myles said. He was giving the
cob of corn in his hands a lot more attention than he
was giving his son. After another close inspection, he
concluded that it needed more butter.

Aaron waited while his father methodically covered
every kernel.

"I can jump almost a foot to what I was jumping
before, dad."

Clare was amazed at his patience, and only by an

act of will did she suppress her maternal instinct to come to his aid. No, it was his show.

"You can do anything you want to do," Myles said, looking at his plate.

Jesus, Katie thought to herself, that man really is a perverse bastard.

"Anyway . . ." Aaron began.

"Pass the pickles," Myles replied, pointing at the dish. Aaron sighed and did what he was told. The "anyway" had torn it: he couldn't go back now, so he might as well get it on.

"Anyway," he repeated, "I want to go to the Olympic trials." It came out faster than he'd intended. So did: "I need two hundred dollars."

Myles, as slowly as he could, returned the unbitten pickle to its dish. So this was it.

"Olympic trials?" he asked, looking from Aaron to Katie to Clare and back to Aaron again. "What Olympic trials?"

"They're on this week in Toronto," Clare broke her silence, speaking almost as quickly as her son. The look Myles gave her was less one of surprise than betrayal.

"George Hayman's authorized my application," Aaron continued, reassured slightly that the odds were now three-to-one, rather than two-to-two, or two-to-one-with-an-abstention.

"I'm making arrangements to go with him," Katie broke her silence. She looked at Clare, and as their eyes locked in, she added: "As his coach."

Myles looked at all three of them, slowly and incredulously. Then he sat back in his chair and picked up the remains of his pickle.

"Well now," he said. "That's just about the craziest thing I ever heard." And that was all he had to say on the matter. They were dismissed. The conversation was over. He bit into the pickle.

Aaron stood. He had tried to be nice, he had tried to make it light and easy. Well, to hell with that.

"I'm only asking for two hundred dollars," he said,

his voice surprisingly even, considering the anger that was building inside him. "I've never asked you for money before."

Myles continued to eat, more noisily now.

Katie squirmed in her chair and wished she were elsewhere.

Clare took a chance: "We'll talk about it, Aaron."

"We're finished talking about it!" Myles was on his feet, pointing a finger at Aaron. The finger was shaking with anger.

"You want to look like a damn fool jumping around on one leg here on the farm—well, that's your business. But I'll be damned if I'll let you make a freak show of yourself in Toronto!" Myles knew instantly he had used the wrong word, and tried to gulp it back—but it was too late. It was the anger. And the anger remained. He would not apologise, not now, not ever.

Aaron came out of his chair so fast that it tipped backwards, and even before he realized what he was doing he kicked it across the room. He took a step toward his father and Myles, as furious as he was, actually took a step back, instinctively bunching his fists. But Aaron stopped, whirled to leave, then whirled again.

"You want to know something?" he screamed, half strangling on the words. "Do you really want to know something? The only one who thinks I'm a freak is my father!" Tears in his eyes, he lurched out the door, letting it bang behind him. Katie, her own fury and frustration about to make her say a few things she might be sorry for, followed him. Myles sat down again and stared gloomily into his coffee.

Clare rose and, without a word, went to the cupboard. Standing on the little three-step ladder, she groped around on the top shelf until she found what she was looking for. She took the jar to the table and unscrewed the lid. Myles continued to look into his coffee.

"You and that boy aren't the only stubborn ones in this house!" she said. "Not by a damn sight." Despite having taken her time in speaking, she did not have her voice fully under control. There were tears in it, and in her eyes.

"He wasn't just asking you for money, you know . . ."

Myles still did not look up, so Clare could not see what was on his face. She assumed it was still anger, but she assumed wrong. It was shame.

Clare counted out $200 from the jar and stuffed it into her apron pocket. She returned the rest of the cash, screwed on the cap and replaced the container up in the cupboard. Behind her she heard Myles' chair scrape. When she turned he was no longer in the room.

In the rapidly-diminishing afterglow, Clare could not quite make out what Aaron and Katie were doing. She left the porch, reaching into her pocket to make sure the money was still there—a lifelong habit—and walked toward them. The canoe, its fresh green paint gleaming in the limited light, was on top of Aaron's car, and he and Katie were lashing it down to the front bumper.

"Where are you taking that?" she asked, beside them now.

"Herb Granger said once he wouldn't mind buying it. I'm going to try and sell it to him," Aaron said, tugging at the bowline knot to ensure it was firm.

"I'll give you two hundred dollars for it," Clare said.

Aaron studied his mother's face, or as much of it as he could see. He didn't respond right away. Finally, when he got his breathing halfway under control, he said: "You? What are you going to do with a canoe?"

"Your father's always saying I need a hobby," she said matter-of-factly. "I've decided on canoeing . . . Of course you'll have to teach me a few of the finer points. When you get back from Toronto."

He took the money without looking at it and stuffed it into his pocket. Clare's hand was still out. "Shake on it?"

"Shake on it," Aaron agreed. Then he put his arms around her and held her for a long, long time.

"Thanks mom," he said at last.

"Okay," Clare said, pretending to become very businesslike. "So get my canoe into the tool shed where it belongs . . . You don't mind, do you, if I use *your* tool shed for *my* canoe?"

As Aaron and Katie began to untie the ropes, Clare reached into the back seat and hauled out the paddle. "I think I'll just hold on to this," she mused. "I've got a feeling I just put myself up the proverbial creek."

11

Aaron and Katie sat on the porch, monitoring the progress of the first full moon of August. After half an hour or so Katie excused herself and went into the house. When she returned a few minutes later, Aaron was standing by his jumping apparatus, reaching up, doing something. As she drew close, she saw that he had moved the crossbar up to seven feet, seven inches.

"Well," he said playfully, "what do you think? Should I do it now or save myself for when it counts?"

"I think," she replied in the same spirit, "that you'd better save yourself . . . How do you feel?"

How did he feel? How *did* he feel? High. Flying. About the same way he felt when he first cleared seven feet. About the same way he felt after the last jump in Montreal, lying there looking up at the crossbar. For the moment he lived in the best of all possible worlds.

"Wonderful," he said. "Wonderful. I almost think I could jump this damn thing. I just can't wait to get going, to get down there."

Katie consulted her watch. "Do you think you can contain all this youthful exuberance for another twelve hours?"

"What's in twelve hours?" he asked.

"Our flight, champ. In case you were wondering what I was doing in the house, I was phoning Air Can-

85

ada. We leave from Saskatoon at 10:15 in the morning.

"And now," she yawned, "I think I'll get myself home, into a shower and into the sack. In case you hadn't noticed, it's been a long day."

"No," he said, "not yet. Just a few more minutes."

"Come on, Aaron, I'm beat. You should be too."

But he wasn't. If anything, he was even higher now. The lovely warm juices of euphoria were running happily through his whole body. He was turned on, in just about every way there is to be turned on.

"Hey. No. Listen. I've got this great idea." It was so great, in fact, that he could not for the life of him understand why he hadn't thought of it before.

"Please, Aaron, make it quick."

He didn't hear the fatigue in her voice. "Listen," he went on, "I've just figured out this great way of saving the COC some money on us. We only get one room at the inn instead of two. What do you think?"

"Very funny," Katie said.

But her inflection was lost on him. "Very practical," he corrected. "It worked just fine in Munich, remember?" The memory increased the stirring in his groin that had begun when he started to get his Great Idea. "Would have worked in Montreal and Edmonton too, if the folks hadn't been there."

Instead of answering, she reached up and put her hand gently over his mouth. His response to that was to take her in his arms, and while she didn't physically resist, she didn't encourage him, either.

"Katie," he whispered into her ear, "you know none of this would have happened without you." He kissed her on the mouth, but she didn't kiss him back, and when he tried to kiss her a second time, she turned her head, deflecting his lips to her cheek.

"Come on, Aaron. Please. Let's call it a night, okay?"

"What's wrong?"

"Nothing. Let's leave it."

"No, goddammit, something's wrong. What is it, the leg?" What a cruel thing to say, he realized instantly.

What a cruel and *stupid* thing to say. Katie had been
looking at that stump every day for weeks now, and it
hadn't bothered her. Or maybe it had. Shit, why did she
have to bring him down like that? It had been so nice
up there. He was a confused man, climbing out of his
damaged ego and not quite sure where he was. Confusion and hurt. All he could think of was hurting back.

"As I recall it," his voice dripped sarcasm, "the leg
is not essential to the act. In fact, though it's been a
long time, I seem to remember that it just got in the
way."

"Goddamn you, Aaron!" She had him by the shirt-
front and she was shaking him. "Goddamn you, listen
to me. I don't deserve this, Aaron, I really don't. And
it's unworthy of you. And to lay the leg business on
me, well, that's even worse. That's bullshit, Aaron!"

"Katie, I'm sorry. It's just that . . ." He couldn't
think of just what.

"You're horny."

"No, it's more than that, I . . ."

"Well, if that's all it is, let's get it on. Up in the
hayloft? It'll seem like old times." Her voice was
brusque, almost businesslike. She would have gone
through with it, he knew that. But he also knew what
she knew: that now he wouldn't.

His silence was her answer. After a few moments
she took his hand in hers and walked him toward the
porch and sat him down.

"Aaron," she began, "I haven't told you this and
I'm not sure why I haven't told you. Anyway, I'm
telling you now." She put her arm around his back
and pulled herself closer. "In Brazil, Greg and I started
going around together. It's funny, isn't it, how you can
know somebody for years and be friends and then, at
some special time in some special place something
happens and you find yourself in love with them. Well
that's what happened, Aaron. I'm in love with Greg
right now, and I'm really looking forward to seeing
him in Toronto."

"But . . ." Aaron was confused. Not hurt any more.
Not rejected. Just confused.

"No," she said, "let me finish. There's something else you should know. When I came back here from Brazil, I didn't intend to stay long. I wanted to see you, very much, and then when I did see you, and everything started to happen so fast, and your mother . . ."

"My mother? What the hell does my mother have to do with all this?"

"Wait, Aaron. Please!"

"No," he said, standing, turning, looking down at her, *"you* wait. Let me tell you what happened. You were going to drop in, say hello, tell me how sorry you were and then bug off to Montreal, right? Up to the mountains, off with those clothes, into the sack, and anybody asks you about good ol' Aaron, well he's coming along, as well as can be expected. Right?"

"Stop it Aaron!"

"But good old mom, she asks you to stick around, to help manage the cripple, and so you do, making this big sacrifice. Well I don't want your pity, Katie, not yours and not anybody's." He started to brush past her into the house, tears in his eyes. If Air Canada was still open he'd call and cancel the flight, cancel everything.

But she stopped him, and held him until he gave up trying to resist.

"Aaron," she said, when she finally had him back sitting beside her. "The only thing you were right about was that I was planning to go off to Montreal. Your mother never tried to make me stay, though I knew she wanted me to. I stayed because I love you and I care about you and I wanted to be with you. I've enjoyed it, Aaron, I really have. It's been exciting and I wouldn't have changed it for anything, wouldn't have traded it for Greg or the Laurentians or anything."

"But," Aaron said, not quite able to read her expression in the moonlight, "I thought you said you were in love with Greg?"

"I am, Aaron, but Greg doesn't run my life. Not Greg, not you, not anybody. I'm my own woman, Aaron, I do what I want to do. I'm grown up and I can make my own choices. I chose to stay here with you, and not go to Montreal. If you ask me why, I guess that right now my need to be needed is greater than my need for a lover. If you ask me why I didn't want to go to bed with you, I guess that I can only handle—only want to handle—one affair at a time. That's what I feel comfortable with."

Again they sat in silence.

"You know I love you, Katie," he said. It was almost a question.

"And I love you. Always have. Always will. But there's one other thing I need from you, Aaron, something more."

"Name it." He was standing, very relaxed and calm. He reached down and pulled her up.

"Understanding," she said. "I need you to understand me."

"Forget it, you tramp."

Her mouth dropped, but only partway. She saw the laughter in his eyes, felt the warmth in his touch.

"Bastard!" she giggled. And kissed him.

Neither Myles nor Clare was asleep. The difference was, he pretended to be. For half an hour, from the time he'd heard her coming upstairs to bed, Myles had lain facing toward the wall, his back to her, not moving, staring at the patches of faded, rose-patterned wallpaper picked up by the square of moonlight that came through the window. He tried not to close his eyes because when he did he started to think, and when he started to think, he started to feel bad. And telling himself that he shouldn't feel bad, that he was right and they were wrong, somehow didn't solve the problem. But the more he stared at that damned wallpaper, the more rapidly it lost its fascination.

Clare, for her part, knew Myles was awake, from his breathing, from his immobility, and from the simple fact that she knew her husband a lot better than he knew himself. He was hurting and confused and ashamed and a few other things, and, being Myles—her beloved, bullheaded Myles—he was almost certain never to admit it. Eventually he would make the adjustments, but he would never acknowledge having done so; Myles hated change, especially in himself. How long had it taken her to get him to sleep in the nude? And it was only months after she'd quit trying that he actually started to do so. Neither of them had ever made mention of it, not in years.

But this time, Clare realized, the process needed to be speeded up. The next couple of days would be, Montreal notwithstanding, the most important in Aaron's life and perhaps in all their lives. She had to talk to Myles, and while she had to do it tactfully, she had to do it now. There was no time to let him come around on his own.

When she heard Katie's car pull away, she knew she had an opener. She also knew it was unworthy of her, a cheap trick. Well, she'd just have to live with it. One deep breath.

"I guess he couldn't talk her into the hayloft," she said, pretending to be musing to herself.

"Clare!"

"Wouldn't have been the first time, you know." Well, that sure got his attention. Myles had rolled over onto his stomach and was struggling to get his elbows tucked under him. There was a look of genuine shock on his face.

"Sometimes I don't believe what comes out of your mouth!"

"I don't know why you're so surprised, Myles. I've been saying what I think for twenty-five years . . . longer." In a second or two she added: "Not like you."

"I meant every word I said to him," Myles insisted. He did just what she'd expected him to do. When he was under attack, even mild attack, he retrenched.

"I know," Clare continued, ignoring his defensive posturing. "It's just not what you were thinking, that's all."

"So now you're a mind reader." It was meant to be grumpy, but it was obvious his heart wasn't in it.

"Only yours, Myles." She swung her body over so that she was half on top of him. She ran her fingers up into the hair on the back of his neck. She snuggled closer and kissed his ear lightly. When she felt him relax, she put her chin on his shoulder and spoke very quietly the words that she would only say—only have to say—once.

"Ever since the accident you've been thinking, 'If only I hadn't . . .' or, 'If only I didn't . . .' It wasn't your fault, Myles, *it wasn't your fault*. Yes, it happened on your farm, with your machine, to your son —but it wasn't your fault." She let that sink in, then continued: "So stop punishing yourself—and stop punishing Aaron. Anybody who didn't know better, they'd think you were angry with him."

"I'm not angry with him." It was a simple statement; he had stopped trying to defend himself.

"Hell," Clare said, "I know that. You love him and you don't want him hurt. So tell him that. You've just got to let people know what's on your mind."

She gripped his hair and turned his head slightly, and with the tip of her tongue licked mischievously at the inside of his ear. Just as mischievously, she whispered, "Like I do . . ."

12

At about the same time that Aaron and Katie were loading up her car for the trip to the airport in Saskatoon, a bellhop was opening the door to Conference Room C of the Margate Inn in downtown Toronto. He motioned to the white-jacketed busboy, who sullenly began carrying silver-colored, Thermos-type coffee pitchers into the room. He spaced three of them evenly along the invisible line that bisected the conference table, then brought in the heavy cups and saucers, the sugar and the cream, and arranged them on the table just as he had been taught to do. He set the two pewter jugs of icy water and the tray of inverted glasses on a side table. He checked his cheap watch against the electric clock that hung at the other end of the room, then pulled out the stem and turned the minute hand back to the correct time: 8:57.

As he started back out the door he was nearly bowled over by a middle-sized, fiftyish man in slacks and an open shirt. The man had not been looking; he was too busy reading something. "Oh . . . uh . . . sorry," the man said, not sounding particularly contrite. "My fault, sir," the busboy said obsequiously. What he wanted to say would have got him fired.

The man poured himself some coffee and read over the papers again. When he looked up, two other men were coming through the door. "Morning, John," said the smaller of the two. His name was Harry Ingram and for a few days back in 1956 he'd been the most famous athlete in Canada, by virtue of an "impossible" gold medal win in the 5,000 meters at Melbourne. The bigger man was James D. Carver Jr., senior vice-president of Sportsgoods International, whose contributions to Canadian amateur sports had made him an almost automatic choice to serve on this executive committee of the Canadian Olympic Committee. "Good morning, Mr. Chairman," he said to John Wallace, the former Nova Scotia cabinet minister whom everybody knew to be the federal government's representative on the committee, and guardian of the funds that the government so grudgingly parted with.

"We may have a problem here, gentlemen," Wallace said, picking up the papers. "But I suppose we'd better wait for the others."

As Aaron went through the electronic safety check at the airport, the buzzer went off. "Excuse me sir," said one of the pimpled young security guards, "could you empty your pockets and try that again?"

"Sure," Aaron replied cheerfully, doing as he was asked. Again there was a loud buzz. The guard wielded the small hand detector lightly over his body. When she got to his right knee the machine began to whine. "What's that?" she demanded.

"What's what?"

By 9:20 Toronto time the six men and two women were all in their places around the conference table. They had finished their greetings, drunk some coffee, and laughed at the joke Philippe Gagnon, Quebec industrialist and vice-chairman of the committee, had heard the night before.

"Ladies and gentlemen," Wallace began, "we have here an application to compete in these current trials. It comes from Aaron Kornylo."

The room was very silent. Even paper-shuffling stopped. "It was in our box here at the hotel when I came in this morning," Wallace continued, "so there was no time to have it Xeroxed. So in essence what it says here is that Kornylo is jumping six-eight, and . . ."

"Amazing!" somebody said.

"Impossible!"

"On one leg? Come on!"

"How does he do it? How can he possibly do it?"

When the room was silent again, Wallace held up the application forms and the letter from George Hayman. "However he does it, he *does* do it. George Hayman has seen him do it, and George recommends him—highly."

"And how high up was the leg severed?" asked Donna Smith, director of women's athletics at the University of British Columbia.

"Well above the knee, I understand," offered Harry Ingram, touching off another round of disbelieving head-shakes.

"Well, gentlemen . . . ladies . . . this is all very interesting, and I'm as pleased as anyone in this room for young Mr. Kornylo. I mean, after all, who can forget what he did in Montreal. But . . ." James D. Carver Jr. held on the "But . . ." giving it a somewhat ominous context. In the business world he was known as a master of the board room, able to get his way as much by his oratorical skills as by the arguments to which he applied them.

"But," he now proceeded, "his participation is something we simply cannot allow." Carver sat down and folded his arms. One of the tricks to getting one's way, he'd learned, was to make a statement and then give the impression that it was the *definitive* statement, that anything that followed was simply superfluous. This time it didn't work.

"Oh, come on, Carver," Ingram said, tossing his pencil at a big empty ashtray with more force than he had intended. "That's ridiculous. The rules don't say a damned thing about one leg or two legs or three. There's nothing . . ."

"You were an athlete, Ingram," Carver interrupted,

"so let me ask you: how would you respond to an amputee?" Before Ingram could reply, Carver answered the question for him: "Guilt, right? Embarrassment? You're thankful it's not you, aren't you, that you're whole?

"Okay," he softened his voice, "now let's be realistic and let's be fair. How can we, in conscience, submit the other competitors to those kinds of emotions on the field? How can they do their best when part of their mind is on Kornylo—no, never mind Kornylo, anybody—and his . . . uh . . . handicap? They couldn't, that's all. That's why we have the Disabled Games."

Ingram recognized the validity of that argument, as much as he disliked its proponent. But his gut told him that Carver was wrong, that there was another argument that would override it. At that very moment, however, he could not come up with one. He glanced around the room. To a man—or woman—everybody was looking down, pretending to read, to pick lint off a cuff, to stir coffee that had been stirred five minutes before. Nobody else had his argument for him. He sat down.

"We have a lot of business to cover today," Wallace said, "so if nobody has anything else to say, I guess we should put it to a vote."

Ingram and Smith voted yes. Carver and four others voted no. Wallace, thankful that he was chairman, didn't vote at all.

"I'd better call George Hayman," Ingram said, getting up. "We're old friends. Maybe Aaron hasn't left yet. Maybe George can head him off." When he left the room he wished the bars were open. Ingram didn't drink very much, but this was one of those times.

Katie and Aaron hadn't been off the ground more than five minutes when the wall phone in the Kornylo kitchen began to ring. In Clare's absence, Myles, who had always harbored a hatred for telephones, reluctantly answered.

After listening a moment: "No, George, I think they're in the air now." He checked with the old kitchen clock. "Yes, definitely . . .

". . . No, I don't know the name of the hotel . . .

". . . No. No, I don't."

"What is it?" Clare asked. The ringing phone had brought her up from the basement, and the tone of her husband's conversation had alerted her that something—something involving Aaron—was wrong.

Myles held up his hand to her, asking her to wait. As he listened further to George Hayman the expression on his face changed from troubled to just plain angry. But he *did* control his voice.

"No . . . no need to apologise, George . . . No, we understand . . . Yes, I'm sure they'll understand too, George. Thanks for calling, George."

"Well?" Clare demanded.

"They're not going to let Aaron compete."

"What! Why not?"

"Didn't say. What's it matter anyway? They say it, that's it . . . I told him not to go."

"Is that all you've got to say?"

"George says there's nothing anybody can do about it."

"Well," Clare said, brushing past him and taking the phone, "I'll be *damned* if I'm just going to sit here." She looked at the white pad in front of her and picked out a number in Katie's handwriting, fresh from the night before. She dialed.

"I'm going to help him," she informed Myles, over her shoulder.

"There's nothing you can do." He was sitting now, trying to figure out if in fact there was anything he, she or anyone else could do.

"I'll think of something." Then, into the phone, she said: "Air Canada? When's the next flight to Toronto?" She listened for a second, then glanced at the clock. "Fine, please make a reservation for one. My name is Kornylo, Mrs. Kornylo. That's K–O–R . . ."

"Make it for two," Myles said, so softly that she almost didn't hear him. "Just a second," she said into the mouthpiece, then, cupping her hand over it, she looked straight at her husband. "What was that?"

"I said: make it for two."

"Excuse me," she said into the phone. "Make that two seats instead of one."

"We'll have to hurry," she said. Myles didn't hear her; he was down in the basement, getting out the suitcases.

Despite the air conditioning, the executive committee—with the exception of Carver, who looked as fresh as he had at nine that morning—was wilting. In a tired voice Wallace presented them with two options. They could stay late and finish the session that night, or they could reconvene in the morning. Either way the business had to get done. Three members had commitments for the next day, and Donna Smith had to fly out first thing in the morning. They agreed to stay. It was 4:45.

The Air Canada ground hostess at Toronto International was just trying to be helpful. When she saw the young man limping along toward the baggage carousel she just naturally went up and offered the services of a wheelchair. Aaron was about to say thanks but no thanks, then reconsidered. He looked at Katie, raising an eyebrow for her opinion. She nodded.

"Thank you," he told the hostess. "That would be very nice. The war, you know." If the hostess heard his throwaway line she pretended not to. She produced the chair and made him comfortable in it. "Shall I take you to the limo?" she inquired.

"Oh, no," said Aaron, "I have a friend with me." He pointed at Katie, who was hauling their bags and his crutches off the carousel.

"Have a good time in Toronto," the girl said, flashing her best professional smile.

"Plan to," Aaron smiled back, gently mimicking her. "By the way, did I tell you I was a one-legged high jumper? Watch this." He began to hop around on his left leg, doing a little jig.

This time the hostess backed away. "You'll have to excuse me," she said, "I have some other work to do." Twice she glanced back as she hurried away, wearing a very confused look.

"Okay, Kornylo, get the hell out of that chair." Katie had her arms and hands full of baggage.

"Yes ma'am," Aaron said. "A gentleman always offers his seat to a lady."

"No, Aaron. Don't be silly."

"Miz Barlow, you've pushed me around long enough. Now it's my turn."

Katie, her lap piled nearly chin-high with suitcases, duffle bags and crutches, watched the people and the shop fronts blur past her, seeing heads turn but quite unable to discern the looks of astonishment she knew had to be on their faces. Faster and faster they tore down the wide, carpeted corridor. Closer and closer loomed the big twin glass doors. She had been very brave, stoic even, but now the irresistable force that was Aaron (and she, and the baggage, and the chair) was about to meet an immovable object. The object, to her great relief, was not immovable. Just as she was screaming, "Aaron!", the doors slid open, and just before they knocked a uniformed Mountie halfway across the driveway, Aaron brought them to a screeching halt. The screeching was his, a poor imitation of automobile brakes.

"Taxi, lady?" he concluded his act.

"My name is Barlow," Katie told the desk clerk, "and this is Mr. Kornylo. We're here for the Olympic trials. I made reservations through Air Canada last night. Two rooms."

While the clerk thumbed through his file cards, and Katie watched him absently, Aaron checked out the lobby for familiar faces. Finding none, he sidled up to Katie, and in a stage whisper, began to berate her.

"So," he said, scrunching up his face in mock anger, "you're really serious about this, are you? You lure me all the way down here from Moose Jaw, destroy my marriage, cost me my friends, my job, and then you tell this man 'two rooms.' Please, Gladys, leave me what's left of my dignity!"

Katie had tried to ignore him, but she couldn't. She looked down, though, because she knew that if she got one look at the desk clerk's face, the laughter she was trying to suppress would just explode into full-blown hysterics. And knowing Aaron, the son-of-a-bitch would just walk away and leave her there with everybody looking at her.

The desk clerk was waiting patiently. They were weird, but he'd seen weirder. "Two rooms, miss."

Katie held up two fingers, and managed a half-strangled, "Yes."

"I wonder," Aaron said, giving the lobby a second glance, "if Carol Coates is here." Katie decided she no longer knew him, and as they followed the bellhop to the elevator she just looked straight ahead and whistled an off-key tune through her teeth.

By the time they reached their eleventh floor rooms, which were side-by-side, she knew him again. "They've got a gym here," she said. "You want to work out?"

Aaron looked at his watch, reset it to Toronto time, and said: "No, it's nearly four o'clock now. Let's get unpacked and then go find something to eat. Anything but a Big Mac."

13

Aaron had never seen Varsity Stadium in late August before, and thus he had never seen it looking its venerable best. Fresh paint gleamed on the seats and on the scoreboard, and the concrete tiers were scrubbed clean. The grass was short and soft and greener than any Aaron had seen for some time, what with the dry spell on the prairies that summer. In the infield two very muscular young men were unleashing discuses while a third man, well downfield, was planting little flags where each discus landed. On the opposite side a couple of workmen in University of Toronto T-shirts were removing a set of hurdles from the track and stacking them against a wall. The long-jump area was deserted, and the only action around the pole-vault area was carried by a track-suited young man and his girl, talking excitedly with their hands and leaning toward one another from time to time for an exchange of kisses.

But somebody was high jumping, and Aaron recognized the form before he was close enough to recognize the man. Katie, however, had known who the jumper was from the moment they'd entered the stadium, and she was running across the field, waving her arms, shouting out his name before Aaron even got a chance to say: "Hey, there's Greg."

"Katie!" Greg met her halfway, even running with his arms wide open.

She leaped into them, revelling in the smell of him, the clean, pure wonderful sweat. She kissed his mouth, she kissed his nose, and she kissed his eyes. She pushed back the dark forelock and kissed his forehead. Then she jumped back and looked at him, her eyes dancing, her smile threatening to break into laughter any second. She cocked her head, and considered her man for a moment. "Nope," she concluded, "I don't care what you say, you still don't look like Michael Douglas."

They swung together again, and when Greg eventually opened his eyes, there was Aaron, looking very self-conscious, pawing the ground with his foot and appearing to be counting his fingers.

"Aaron! Well hi. I didn't think you guys would be here. It's good to see you both." What he really meant was that it was good to see Katie. A couple of short phone conversations over two thousand-odd miles had not tended to put his mind at ease about the kind of relationship these two were sharing. Besides, he hadn't talked to her for weeks. But the way Katie felt in his arms, the way she'd kissed him, told him that what they'd started in Brazil was, despite the time lag and the somewhat strange intervening circumstances, apparently still in operation.

Aaron was damned if he was going to look uncomfortable. "How are you doing?" he asked, with just the right degree of brightness.

Greg reached over Katie's shoulder and extended his hand to Aaron, who shook it heartily. He was, in fact, glad to see Greg. They'd jumped a few crossbars and downed a few beers together in the last five years, and while he still had some problems putting Greg and Katie together in his mind, despite the firsthand evidence, it still felt good, standing by the uprights with his friend and peer again.

"Sorry about what happened, Aaron," Greg said as he and Katie extricated themselves from one another. "Hell of a thing. I was going to call, or write or something. I even started a letter . . . but it just seemed

. . . it just seemed . . . not enough. You know what I mean?"

"Sure, Greg," Aaron replied. And he did.

"Anyway," Greg changed the conversation, "are you here to see me win the high jump?"

Before Aaron could answer, Katie said quickly: "I'm . . . uh . . . coaching high jump."

Aaron could see the puzzlement on Greg's face. He's trying to figure out who, Aaron thought. He's wondering if somewhere out there in God's Country she's found some other big farmboy who's half-gazelle. He decided to let Katie handle it for a while longer.

"Who?" Greg asked her. "Who are you coaching?"

"Why, Aaron of course."

"Aaron? But . . ."

Aaron gave him an ah-shucks look.

"Aaron. *You're* jumping?"

"It's a living," Aaron said offhandedly.

"But . . . I mean, that's great! Fantastic." Then the look of puzzlement returned. "But how?"

"Straight dive," Aaron replied.

"Simple—but it works," Katie added.

Greg tried to visualize it, but couldn't. "When do we see it?" he asked.

"Do you want to try it now?" Katie asked Aaron.

He toyed with the possibility. His gear was in the dressing room under the stadium, and it wouldn't have taken him more than ten minutes to get dressed and back out there. "Better not," he decided finally. "It might look so good everybody will go out and lose a leg just to try it out. Naah, I'll wait."

"Right," Greg said, still not 100 percent convinced these two rustics weren't just putting the city boy on. He studied Katie's eyes for an indication of that, and found something else, something quite different, something that very quickly took his mind other places.

"Katie . . ." he said.

It was Aaron who answered. "Listen," he said, "why don't we all go somewhere intimate, where you two can talk, okay? And then when I get bored . . ."

Before either of them could answer he was wandering off toward the exit, waving without looking back.

Greg and Katie sat in the dark comfortable lounge at the Moorings, sipping white wine, effectively hidden from the rest of the world in big, side-by-side wing back easy chairs. For the past hour she'd talked about little other than Aaron. Her enthusiasm was not infectious, and despite the earlier indications Greg was now wondering—worrying, even—about where exactly he was placed in Katie's scheme of things.

"You never answered my letters," he interjected, bringing the conversation around to where he wanted it—or at least where he thought it should be. "Why didn't you call me or something?"

"I've been busy with Aaron," she said simply.

"How busy?" It was half a question, half an accusation.

"Busy." She knew what he was trying to get at.

"Permanently busy?"

"Dammit, Greg, don't give me the third degree. He needed me and I was there. When he doesn't need me any more, I'll leave. If that's not enough for you now, well I just can't help it."

Greg wasn't sure if it was enough. He remembered what she'd told him in Brazil as they lay together in the hotel room and listened to the pre-dawn sounds of the farm people setting up their markets in the street below. "I won't be owned," she had said. That and a few other things that could have been passed off as youthful bravado. He hadn't quite believed her then. Now, with some reluctance, he was beginning to.

But he didn't want to get into it. The trials were only hours away and they demanded his full emotional attention. Besides, she was his right now, even if it did seem to be on a short-term lease.

"Why don't we go back to the hotel?" he said.

"Why M'sieur Dubois," she replied coquettishly, "I've heard that athletes were supposed to be pure in both mind and body—especially the night before the big game."

"Tell it to Joe Namath," he laughed, dropping three dollars and change on the tray to cover their bill.

As they walked along Yonge Street, a polite young man with a beatific smile handed Katie a rose and began to talk to the two of them as if they were the nicest, most beloved people it had ever been his pleasure to meet. Before he could get very far, Greg began shouting at him in French, gesturing wildly and pointing at something across the street. Before the kid could compose himself, Greg was steering Katie quickly up the sidewalk.

"Goddamned Hare Krishna," he muttered.

"Oh?" she said in a small voice, "but I thought they shaved their heads and wore those funny robes."

"Disguises now," Greg said.

"What did you say to him? It sounded brutal."

"I just asked him the directions to Bloor Street," Greg laughed. "Then I asked him if that was his mother standing over there in that doorway. Works every time."

They were passing a place called Funland, where just about every kind of coin-operated amusement known to man was blasting various dings, buzzes, whirrs, and rat-a-tats out into the street. "Look," Katie motioned. "There's Aaron."

"Yeah," Greg said, taking her arm and attempting to steer her away from the pinball parlor and back to the hotel for some less juvenile recreation. "Listen, Katie, there's an ancient rule that you don't disturb a man when he's playing pinball. Makes him lose his concentration. See. See how intense he is."

"Oh, let's go in for a few minutes. Besides, he's not playing pinball, he's shooting some kind of rifle or something."

Aaron, as Luke Skywalker, was blasting the Imperial Storm Troopers out of the void, hopping around like a kid at the fair, oblivious to everybody and everything around him. On one of these swings through deep space his hip banged against the pinball machine beside him, a brand new entry into the field of noise and color featuring Hugh Hefner and his girls and called, appropriately, Playboy. The frizzed blonde at the flippers was in no mood for this kind of intrusion: in an hour she hadn't broken 100,000 and it took 220,000 to win. Now this hyperactive jerk had tilted the damn thing just when she was starting to get somewhere.

"Hee-eey, cowboy, you tilted my machine!" Allowing Darth Vader to escape once more, Aaron gave her his less than undivided attention. "The machine!" she told his blank face. "The machine! You tilted it! Ruined my game. You know?" Aaron just continued to look as, in his mind, he put together "machine" and "tilt" and "game."

"You weren't doing very well," he observed.

"I was doing just fine," she said. "Besides, you tilted it and you owe me a quarter."

"You get two games for a quarter," Aaron said, having fully returned from other galaxies by now. "I only tilted one."

The girl, who, Aaron was now able to notice, had a more than passably pretty face and an even more passably pretty body, raised an eyebrow in incredulity. This guy was obviously some kind of nut. Or this was some kind of goof. Or both. "You're going to offer me twelve-and-a-half cents! I don't believe it."

Aaron fished into his pocket. "Of course I wouldn't offer you twelve-and-a-half cents," he said. "Here's thirteen. You can give me my change later."

By this time Katie and Greg were standing behind the combatants, with Katie trying to decide who needed rescuing the most and Greg trying to decide on a plan of action that would get him and Katie out of there undetected.

"In fact," Aaron continued, "I'll even stake you to another dime. There's a machine over there . . ." He turned to point, saw Katie and Greg, smiled and carried on. "There's a machine over there that says it'll test your intellect for a dime. From what I've seen, that's about all it's worth."

The girl looked up at him, a mixture of mock

fright and real contempt in her eyes. "Ooohh," she said, "that's macho. Ve-ry macho. Next you're going to hit me, right?"

"I told you we shouldn't have let him out on his own," Katie said to Greg, loudly and with overstated resignation in her voice.

"Yes," Greg said, picking up her cue and shaking his head sadly. "It does seem to happen every time, doesn't it. Come on now, Aaron, let's not make any more trouble, shall we?"

Katie handed the girl a quarter and an apology, and she and Greg took Aaron firmly by the arms and walked him toward the door. Aaron turned to the girl, who was alternately looking at the departing trio and the quarter in her hand, an expression of confusion on her face. "I was not always as you see me now," Aaron shouted, rolling his eyes and letting his mouth hang open and his tongue loll. The girl did not return to her game until she was sure they were safely gone.

14

Even before the elevator doors had closed, Clare had read the signs on the opposite wall, and was steering her husband to the left.

"What if the meeting's over?" she asked.

"Don't know," Myles answered.

Their luggage was still down in the lobby. They hadn't even checked in yet. The sign downstairs had said the executive committee was meeting from 9 A.M. to 5 P.M., but the commissionaire, a crinkly old man with World War II ribbons on his chest, had told them that he hadn't seen anybody leave, or at least come back down to the lobby. He made a point of noticing these things, he said; it helped pass the time. Besides, he'd recognized Harry Ingram when the former runner had come in three days before and was still looking for an opportunity to walk up and shake the man's hand and maybe even ask for an autograph.

As Myles and Clare walked noiselessly through the thick hall carpet to Conference Room C, she reached out for his hand and squeezed it. He squeezed back. And that's the way they arrived at the door.

Aaron walked Katie and Greg to the elevator and waited with them for it to arrive. "I don't know whether to thank you or not," he told them. "I might have scored back there."

"Well," said Greg, "you sure looked like you were on the way."

"Best come-on I ever heard," Katie added. "Here's the elevator. We'll see you later."

Aaron wandered off toward the smoke shop, thinking he might as well pick up a magazine or something. Then he thought about the girl at Funland. What the heck, he wouldn't mind trying that machine she was playing anyway. Ahh, she was probably gone by now . . . well, maybe she wasn't. Maybe he could ask her what a nice girl like her was doing in a place like this. She was gone. But he played the machine anyway, winning three games on his second try.

"Well," Wallace was saying to the tired faces around the conference room table, "we've done pretty well today. One more item and we're finished, and it's just six-twenty. Now, do I . . ."

"Excuse me," Myles said. He and Clare left the doorway where they had stood unnoticed for about ten seconds and arrived, side by side, at the table. Seven weary faces, plus James Carver's, looked up at them inquiringly.

"There wasn't anybody outside," Clare said. "Are you in charge here?" she asked Carver.

"No," he answered. Technically that was true.

"I'm the chairman of the committee," Wallace said, standing up and listlessly extending his hand to Clare and Myles. "My name is Mr. Wallace. May we help you?"

"My name is Clare Kornylo. This is my husband, Myles. What we want to know is why you're not letting our boy Aaron compete."

Silence. Shuffling. Expulsions of breath.

"We gave your son's application due consideration," Wallace said finally. He had withdrawn his hand when it had not been acknowledged, and he was doing his talking to the surface of the table.

"The decision wasn't an easy one," said Donna Smith, who was not afraid to meet Clare's eyes. She wanted to say that she and Harry Ingram had voted for Aaron, but this committee had an unwritten code: a majority vote automatically became a unanimous vote; no dissension could ever be seen, no split in the ranks, no "good guys" and "bad guys."

"We've come to find out why," Clare said.

"Mrs. Kornylo . . ." Carver stood and walked around the table. He had an apologetic little smile on his face. Actually, he didn't feel the least bit apologetic, but they didn't have to know that. Casually he sat on the table edge. Then, making a point of talking directly to Clare, he explained, like some indulgent parent, the facts of life to her.

"Mrs. Kornylo, you must appreciate that it is our responsibility to weigh all the circumstances of every application and then come to a decision which is in the best interests of everybody—the competitors, the committee, amateur athletics in general. I'm sure you and your husband here understand that. And I'm sure that you also understand that this particular meet—these trials—will determine our team, at least in part, for the 1980 Olympics in Moscow. Now, Mrs. Kornylo . . ."

Clare backed off a half step, and the movement was not lost on Carver. "Now, Mrs. Kornylo . . ."

"Why did you reject my son?" Myles was between them, his face not six inches from Carver's.

Wallace saw Myles' clenched fists. He saw the color rising out of the too-tight white collar. He saw Myles' eyes become slits. He heard the tremble of anger in the voice. "There are other competitions for Aaron, Mr. Kornylo." He wasn't being conciliatory. He was being scared. Myles was the biggest man in the room, and he was an unknown quantity so far as reactions were concerned. What if this big farmer started hitting people?

"This is the only one that counts right now," Myles said, all manifestations of anger intact.

"I . . . uh . . . understand, Mr. Kornylo."

"Do you, Mr. . . . what is it? . . . Wallace? Do you, Mr. Wallace?" Then: "Have you seen him jump?"

Wallace gave his head a little shake. Carver had

taken the opportunity to move down the table and out of harm's way. For the first time he too was looking down. Clare took another step backward: Myles was handling this, and doing so to her liking.

"Have any of you seen him jump?" Myles asked, looking at each person individually. Only Harry Ingram looked back at him.

"We've seen the statistics," Carver answered. He had his composure again, or at least its façade.

"And they say he qualifies."

"There are other considerations, Mr. Kornylo."

These bastards, Myles thought, have an answer for everything. Okay, let them answer this: "He can jump your required height, he's registered and he's experienced—not to mention the fact that he did you awful proud in Montreal. He has every right to try."

Carver sensed, as did Myles, that it was just the two of them now, that everybody else in the room was merely part of an audience.

"Yes," Carver exhaled, "he does have the right to jump . . ." Nine pairs of eyes were now on him, all of them slightly bewildered. "Except when it interferes with the well-being of the other athletes." The nine pairs of eyes were still on him, but the bewilderment had left them. "We believe your son—your son's presence in the trials—would represent a . . . uh . . . diversion to them."

"You mean a freak show . . ." It was the second time in less than twenty-four hours that Myles had used those words, a fact that was not lost on him. God, how he'd wished, the night before and all that long disorienting day, that he had said something else or, better, nothing at all. But this occasion at least partially made up for the first: it wasn't just Carver he was punishing with sarcasm, or the committee. It was himself.

"Now, Mr. Kornylo . . ." Carver began.

But Myles wasn't listening any more. He wasn't even looking at these people any more. He'd had about enough of their stupid excuses and he'd had about enough of their stupid faces. He took Clare's elbow and together they walked out the door. In a few moments Wallace went over, looked up and down the hall a little nervously, closed the door and returned to the table.

"Maybe we could reopen it?" Ingram suggested.

"No," Carver said, "it's been settled. We have other business here. Now where were we before we were so . . . uh . . . rudely interrupted?"

"The food concession business," Wallace said.

"Ah yes," said Carver. "Well, we simply tell them to stay off the field during the trials, that's all. After all, this is an Olympic event, not some carnival. Can we have a vote, Mr. Chairman . . ."

Aaron looked damned good, if he did say so himself, in his grey slacks and polished boots, his crested Olympics blazer and light blue shirt and the neat red-and-black silk tie he'd bought in Montreal. The comb didn't do much for his unruly blond curls, but then it never had, had it? He was saved from total self-absorption by Katie's knock at the door.

"Hi," she said. "You're lookin' good, Kornylo."

"So are you, coach. Looks to me like you and Greg have managed to get things squared away."

"Does it show that . . . uh . . . we're working on it?"

"So it seems." Both were enjoying the little game they were playing, and the fact that once more their relationship was devoid of tensions, sexual or otherwise.

As they strolled down the hall to the elevators, Aaron thought of something. "By the way, Katie, do you know if Carol Coates *is* here?"

"Forget it, farmboy. She'd eat you up alive."

"That's sort of what I had in mind."

"You find them okay?" the commissionaire asked as Claire and Myles re-emerged into the lobby.

"We found them," Clare said, "but it wasn't okay."

"Where do we check in?" Myles asked.

While Clare filled out the registration, Myles wandered back to the commissionaire, first to apologise for his abruptness a few minutes before, and second to find out, if possible, where the executive committee members were staying. The old man led him to a display table in the foyer and then handed him a mimeographed program. On the last page were the names, Toronto addresses (four of the members lived in the city, the others were in hotels) and telephone numbers.

"Guess I can take this," Myles said.

The old man nodded.

Myles rejoined Clare at the front desk. "You get him?" he asked.

"Room doesn't answer."

"Katie?"

"Same thing. Guess we might as well go up and unpack."

"You go ahead, dear." The word surprised both of them. "You go ahead, Clare," Myles amended. "Oh, and get yourself a bite to eat. It's going to be a long night."

"Don't you want to change first?"

"No. There'll be plenty of time for that later."

She watched his back disappear through the revolving door, and even when she couldn't see him any longer, she remained oblivious to the bellboy, standing beside her with their bags in either hand.

"Give 'em hell, darling," she whispered.

Myles' first stop was the Windsor Arms Hotel, where Donna Smith was staying. He had to hit the out-of-town people first, just in case some or all of them were heading back that night.

"I believe I saw Ms. Smith go into the Courtyard Cafe," the desk clerk said.

"Where's that?"

"Just go through those doors and make a left."

"Thank you."

If Myles had been the least bit open to intimidation that night, the Courtyard and its "beautiful people" clientele would have overwhelmed him. But he had other things—one other thing—on his mind, and he didn't even notice when the maitre d' gave his conservative old grey suit and his Saskatchewan haircut the critical onceover.

"I'm looking for a Miss Smith," he said. "A Miss Donna Smith," he corrected, recognizing that even this wasn't much of a description. "The manager said she was here."

"Ah yes," said the maitre d', "the lady from Vancouver. I'll show you to her table." The beautiful people didn't even look up at Myles as he passed. They were too busy being witty. Or bored.

"Miss Smith?" He'd hardly noticed her in the committee room, but he did now. She was striking. Katie, ten years later.

"Mr. Kornylo? Won't you sit down?"

"Thank you," he said, sliding self-consciously into the booth. "I think you know why I'm here."

Donna Smith put her Caesar's salad to one side. She sipped her Chablis and regarded the seamed, honest face across the table from her.

"Mr. Kornylo," she began, "our committee has a rule, which I'm about to break . . ."

Aaron and Katie hesitated in the doorway of the banquet room, peering into the muted light for old friends, or, at least, old acquaintances.

"There he is," Greg Dubois nudged the tall, gangling man beside him.

Steve Catlow looked toward the doorway, then back at Greg. "No crutches," he said, loudly enough to make Greg wince. The two men had three things in common: their age, their comfortable background, and their ability to jump high in the air. In fact, with Aaron apparently out of the way, it was a toss up as to which of them was the best in the country; Greg had beaten Steve in Brazil, by half an inch, but earlier in the year, at the Maple Leaf Indoor Games, Catlow had come within the same distance of tying Aaron's Canadian record. Steve was nonetheless a fool, and Greg did not suffer him gladly. He even found himself irritated by Steve's appearance: no matter what time of year it was, Steve Catlow looked like he trained in a closet; from his hair to his skin to the clothes he wore, he was beige. Greg once asked Aaron, who tended to have good (and devastating) one-word descriptions, if there was any term for a beige albino. But this time, Aaron couldn't help.

"No crutches?" Steve repeated.

"Prosthesis," Greg replied. When he saw the lack of comprehension in Steve's face, he simplified. "Artificial leg."

"*I* knew that," Steve lied. He watched Katie and Aaron begin their circle of the room. He waved, but they didn't see him. Then he turned back to Greg. "You sure he can jump?"

"He says he can, and Katie says he can, so I guess he can. He had to do six-eight to get here."

Steve was still keeping an eye on Aaron's progress around the ballroom, and Greg could almost see the wheels turning in his head, trying to figure what a one-legged high jump looked like.

"Do you know how he does it?" Steve asked.

"Straight dive," Greg replied. Actually, he'd been having trouble picturing it himself. "I know what you're thinking," he added. "That it's illegal. But it isn't."

Steve shook his head. "No," he said, "I wasn't thinking that. I was thinking that . . . I was just thinking if it happened to me—losing a leg like that, you know—I mean I doubt if *I'd* be here. I mean I don't think I'd want anybody to see me. How about you, Greg? The same for you, right?"

Greg couldn't bring himself to answer, only because he'd grown weary of meaningless questions. Steve Catlow was a pain in the ass, sometimes more than others. This was one of those sometimes. Greg was about to excuse himself and catch up with Aaron and Katie, but then the cavalry arrived in the person of Carol Coates, accompanied by a familiar-looking blonde girl. Now where had he seen her before . . . ?

"Hello, lover," Carol said, sliding her hands up Greg's chest and kissing him on the mouth. She stayed there about a second too long, just time enough for his face to start to redden and for his eyes to start searching for Katie, to see, God forbid, if she'd been watching. Carol, sensing his discomfort, played her game for another couple of beats, winked him an overstated wink, and slid down.

The pretty blonde girl kept her head down. She hung it further when Catlow, who'd finally figured out that he and Greg had visitors, boomed, "Carol Coates! Thank God you're here," and called down the attention of about a quarter of the people in the room.

Carol turned slowly, squaring her Bacall shoulders, pushing back her Bacall hairstyle, and growling in her Bacall voice. "Hello, Steve," she said. "Still exuding that quiet charm, I see."

"Ever since Montreal," Steve continued, her put-down lost on him, "I've had this pain. Right here." He thumped at his chest. If he means his heart, Greg thought, he's off by half a foot.

"Jesus," Carol replied, adding even more Bacall to her voice, "I hope it's nothing trivial."

The blonde girl touched her lightly on the arm.

"Oh, Christ," Carol said, "I'm sorry. Gentlemen, I would like you to meet Tricia McMahon, who is from Edmonton, and who is not one of *the* McMahons, if you know what I mean." Greg nodded, connecting the name McMahon to oil wells and the city's major sports stadium; Steve looked blank.

"And these, Tricia, are Greg Dubois, who is not a total swine, even if he did stand me up in Rio de Janeiro—the fool—and Steve Catlow. They . . . uh . . . jump. It's a silly sport, but these two are very good at it."

Tricia's grey eyes, which had been hesitant, began to light up. "I know," she said. "I've seen them." She studied Greg for a moment, then suggested, just a touch shyly: "I think we almost met earlier today. At the pinball place."

"I knew it," Greg said, reaching out to shake her hand. "I knew I'd seen you before. You're the girl with the tilted machine."

Carol looked a little mystified.

"And you were my savior," Tricia said. "You and that girl. Who was that nut anyway, the one with the mouth and the limp?"

Greg was about to defend Aaron, but then he figured what the hell, Aaron *was* a nut. "You mean you don't know?" he said instead. "If you watched the '76 Olympics at all, you probably saw him win the bronze medal. Or if you were at Edmonton last summer, you saw him beat me and Catlow here out of the gold. That's Aaron Kornylo. He's right over there."

Tricia's face reddened. She'd seen both: Montreal on TV and Edmonton in person. "But," she said, looking from Greg to Carol and back, "he lost his leg, didn't he? What's he doing here, coaching or something or just watching?"

"Competing," Greg said. He half-prayed nobody would ask him how Aaron did it.

"Competing?" Carol growled. "How does he do it?"

While Greg explained, Tricia sought Aaron in the direction Greg had nodded, and spotted him and the girl, shaking hands with a young man at the far end of the room who looked to be part, maybe full, North American Indian. Tricia watched Aaron's lips moving, and his hands waving, and she saw the Indian begin to laugh and shake his head and touch Aaron lightly on the chest. She wondered if that was Aaron's girl, or whether she belonged to this fellow Greg.

"So," Greg was now saying, "what do you do, Tricia?"

"Pardon? Oh . . . I . . . uh, work in a bank back home. And I go to night school."

"No, no," Catlow interjected. "We want to know what you do in track and field."

"The hundred meters," she replied. She wasn't looking at Catlow, but rather at the increasingly-fascinating man with the limp, who was now shaking hands with the Indian for a second time and moving on past him.

"Some of my best friends are sprinters," Steve allowed, putting his arm around Tricia's shoulders.

"Some of my best friends are high jumpers," Carol said, as Tricia stood there looking uncomfortable and not quite knowing what to do about it. "Greg here, for example. And Aaron."

"I'd like to meet this Aaron," Tricia said, trying not to sound too enthusiastic, but betraying herself anyway.

"I bet you would," Carol replied with a hokey leer. "Come on, I'll introduce you. Oh, and don't worry about the girl with him, she's Greg's. Or Greg is hers. Or whatever . . ."

Myles waved down a cab on Bloor Street. "Do you know where the Royal York Hotel is?" he asked the driver.

"Sure do, mister."

The streetlights and the neon and the glow coming through the windows of the still-open stores of Yonge Street allowed him to read once more the letter Donna Smith had handwritten for him on her own notepaper. It was addressed to John Wallace and it said, in part, "While I have always respected the policy of the committee concerning unanimity, I feel that in this particular case I must make an exception. I therefore vote that Aaron Kornylo be allowed to compete and I urge that you and the other members of the committee do likewise . . ."

Myles studied his list. Gagnon next and then Ingram, who, Smith had assured him, would be easy.

15

Whenever James D. Carver Jr. entered a room, all eyes turned to him. Or so he fancied. Back in 1968, when the word "charismatic" was still being lavished on Prime Minister Pierre Elliott Trudeau by the media pack, Carver had begun studying the way people reacted to him, and decided that whatever the prime minister had, he had too.

Which was the main reason he'd stayed around the Margate after the committee session ended, to have his charisma reaffirmed. That's not what he'd said, of course. What he'd said was that at least one member of the committee should stay around to mix with the athletes at the dinner and dance, and that he had nothing on that night anyway. He'd also said that, as the principal objector to Aaron Kornylo's participation in the trials, he'd be the one to tell the boy.

Now, freshly showered, his handsome face still pink from his second barber-shop shave of the day, his dark blue Bill Blass silk suit hanging on his lean body perfectly, Carver stepped confidently into the ball room. And sure enough, about half of the inhabitants either turned to look, or at least cast sideways glances. He answered waves with smiles and smiles with waves. But tonight, for some reason, his effect wasn't total, and it didn't take long to see why. Carver followed the eyes of the people immediately around him, and saw what —or rather whom—they were looking at.

Kornylo.

For just a part of a second, the smile left Carver's face. Then he caught it and brought it back. Kornylo. Seeing the boy, actually *seeing* him, had suddenly made Carver's self-imposed task seem a little harder than he'd thought it would be. It was obvious, from the way the boy was laughing and gesturing, that he didn't know yet, that he hadn't run into his parents. Or if he had, they hadn't told him.

Carver touched the knot of his tie, decided it was a little loose, and adjusted it. What was he going to do about Kornylo? It didn't seem proper, did it, to approach the kid in this roomful of people? No point in making a scene. Besides, the kid had a coach, didn't he? It was more proper to tell the coach, anyway; it was better form. Now, what was the guy's name? No, it wasn't a guy, it was a girl, probably that good-looking dark-haired one with Kornylo now. Katie Barlow? Yes, that's right. A hurdler or something.

But later. When the crowd had thinned.

"Isn't that Carver over there, from the committee?" Aaron nudged Katie. The man was now hidden behind a couple of weight lifters. Or if they weren't weight lifters, they should have been.

"Can't tell," Katie said. "But there's the ever-popular Carol Coates over there, talking to Greg and the ever-unpopular Steve Catlow. Oh-oh, Aaron, she's spotted us. Better start saying your prayers."

"My prayers have been answered already," Aaron said. "Look, they're coming over here."

"Aaron!" Carol greeted him with a kiss. "Is it ever good to see you here. You too, Katie, even if you did steal the man I wanted to be the father of my children . . . Aaron, how are you?"

"Couldn't be better. Hello again Greg. Hi Steve, I see you found your way back from Brazil. Congratulations on your jumping, by the way, I hear my old record was almost in trouble. And who is this young lady? I have the feeling we've met before." Aaron had prepared the speech while the four were crossing the floor, and his attempts at spontaneity showed as much.

"I'm Patricia McMahon. Tricia. From Edmonton. Hello, Aaron. Katie." Her voice was small and shy. Her hand was dry and warm in his, and he was in no hurry to release it. Nor did she appear anxious to have it released.

"I'd like to apologise," Aaron said, almost as shyly.

As Tricia attempted to compose an answer that would not embarrass either of them, Steve Catlow elbowed his way into the conversation.

"So, Aaron, how do you do it?"

"Charm," Aaron replied. "Pure, unadulterated charm."

"Umm," Tricia murmured. Then, realizing where she was and what she was doing—what she had done —she cursed herself and tried to will away the crimson that was taking over her cheeks. This time she was thankful for Steve Catlow.

"No," Steve persisted, moving between her and Aaron, "you know what I mean."

Aaron had spent so many years learning to tune out Steve Catlow that he'd almost succeeded. So he had to remember again just what Steve was talking about. Oh, yeah. He took a step to the left before he answered. He was more interested in seeing the blonde girl than the beige bore.

"It's sort of a combination," he explained. "Roll and dive."

"But isn't that illegal?"

"Goddamnit, Catlow," Greg groaned, rolling his eyes heavenward in a silent prayer for deliverance, "I just told you it wasn't!"

"Not if you take off on one foot," Katie came to the rescue.

"Oh," Catlow said, rubbing his chin wisely. "So what height have you made?"

Greg groaned again.

"He'll show you tomorrow," Katie said. "Hey, they're starting to serve dinner. Let's grab a table."

• • •

"Ah, Mr. Kornylo. I am not surprised to see you."
Philippe Gagnon ushered Myles into his suite.

"You're not?" Myles asked.

"No, m'sieur, I am not. I like to think that I can tell
about people, and when I saw you earlier this evening
I thought to myself: 'this is a determined man, this is
a man who will not stop.' But never mind that. You
are here to see me to ask if I will vote to have your
son compete.

"I will save us both a lot of time. I have a note right
here. And Mr. Kornylo . . ."

"Yes?"

"Bonne chance."

Between the overcooked roast beef and what looked
suspiciously like custard lumps, Carol and Tricia made
a pilgrimage to the lady's john.

"Well," Carol said as they adjusted themselves in
front of the two big mirrors, "I take it that our Aaron
hasn't been a disappointment, at least not so far."

"He's . . . uh . . . very attractive, isn't he?"

Tricia ever-so-carefully replenished her lipstick and
Carol impatiently pushed at her short shiny bangs with
her fingers. "Yeah, and he's a pretty good guy, too.
Funny guy. I was worried that maybe the accident
would change him, but it hasn't. That Dennis Weaver
routine was hilarious, wasn't it?"

"Yeah. I only wish I hadn't been so dumb, though.
I mean I thought Dennis Weaver was McCloud. I
never heard of Chester until just now. Did you know?"

"Yes, but then I had a wasted youth. Listen, do you
want me to arrange it so you two can be alone?"

Tricia did, of course, but it was not such an easy
thing to admit.

"Don't worry, kid. Greg and Katie will be pairing
off together, and I'll take care of Catlow. He's a boor
and a moron, but there's one thing he's good at. And I
haven't had any for nearly two weeks. God!"

When Harry Ingram told Myles Kornylo he would
be right down, he meant *right down*. Myles hadn't

even made it across the admittedly vast lobby of the
Harbour Castle hotel when Ingram was running up to
his side. "Always take the stairs," he explained, breathing easily. "Below ten floors I can still whip most
elevators."

He handed Myles two envelopes, one open and
one sealed. "Donna called me, and I know how valu-
able your time is right now. The open one has my yes
vote. The other one has my resignation. I hope you
don't have to deliver the second one, but if you do,
I'm damned proud to have *you* do it."

Myles started to speak, but the lump in his throat
interfered.

"I won't keep you, Mr. Kornylo, but there's a story
I think you should know. When I was a boy, growing
up on the farm—just like Aaron, I believe—we read
this story in public school. It was about a kid named
Glenn Cunningham, who had his legs really badly
burned in a fire when he was really small. They said
he'd never walk again, but you know what? He became
the best middle distance runner of his time. He was my
hero, Mr. Kornylo. I'm forty-one years old now and
he's still my hero. You tell Aaron that story, okay?"

Myles still hadn't spoken, and before he could even
get his mouth open Ingram was sprinting for the
stairs.

"Okay," Myles finally mumbled.

To everybody's everlasting gratitude Steve Catlow
had been remarkably quiet throughout the meal. It
was hard to talk, of course, with his mouth full, and
that had been his ongoing condition. Steve actually
liked the food, and the other five had generously loaded
and reloaded his plate from theirs.

But as they left the banquet room for the strobe
lights and sounds of The BeeGees and *Saturday Night
Fever,* next door, he started up again on Aaron. "You
over six-and-a-half?" he asked through a mouthful of
colored mints.

"I told you. You'll see tomorrow," Katie said.

"You heard the coach," Aaron added.

"So what's all the mystery?" Steve wanted to know.

"The mystery," Carol Coates explained, taking his arm, "is why you're talking when you could be dancing. Come on."

Greg and Katie followed suit. Aaron and Tricia stood together in awkward silence, each of them searching for a combination of words that wouldn't sound too silly or too obvious or too trite. As usual Aaron's mastery of the language prevailed. "Want a drink?"

She shook her head. "Want to dance? Ohhh! I'm sorry. I . . ."

"No, don't be. I can take a canoe through raging rapids—well, almost—and I can leap tall crossbars at a single bound, so maybe I can actually dance, too. Don't know about my wooden leg, though. I usually leave him behind." But he was a little worried. Everybody had been watching him when he was just walking, and he could feel the eyes again as he led Tricia out onto the dance floor. He wished he felt as confident as he sounded.

But with Tricia's encouragement—once she started to move, to twist and slide to the rhythms—he found himself getting happily lost in the music, which, to be frank, he didn't even particularly like. At first he favored the right leg, or the prosthesis, a little too much, bending only to the left. But after a few minutes out there, he tested the hydraulics of the artificial joint, and a few minutes after that he was just about matching Tricia's sensual gyrations.

"How are you doing?" she shouted over the din.

"John Travolta, eat your heart out!" he shouted back.

"Your leg doesn't hurt?"

"Only when I laugh . . . Sorry about that."

Myles checked his watch, which was the only piece of jewelry he owned other than the plain gold wedding band; Aaron had bought him that watch, brought it back from Germany in 1972 for Myles' fortieth birthday. He held his wrist up in the light. It was a few minutes after ten and he still had three more people to see. Tannenbaum was next, then Wallace, then Carver. If that Barbara Dodds woman hadn't been such a pain in the ass at first . . .

"This is the place, Mr. Kornylo," the cabbie said, pointing to the huge stone edifice on the right. "You want me to wait again, right?"

The meter now read $47.60.

"Yes," Myles said. "Please."

Something woke Clare. A slammed door down the hall, a honking horn outside, something. The room was dark. Instinctively and tentatively she said: "Myles?" Dammit, she hadn't meant to sleep; she had just stretched out for a moment, and now who knew what time it was. No watch, no clocks, no radio. She vacillated between calling the front desk and trying to get something on the TV that would give her the time. She opted for the latter. On one channel a teleprinter was writing the news on a blue backdrop, and down in the right-hand corner a set of numbers said it was 10:17:34 . . . 35 . . . 36 . . . But where on earth was Myles? And Aaron? She had to get up and do something. No, wait. Myles was handling things, wasn't he?

She dressed in the best clothes she had with her, which were also the best clothes she owned. On the back of a hotel envelope she wrote, in neat block letters, "Myles. In the bar. See you soon. Love. C," licked the glue on the flap and stuck it to the outside of the door.

While Aaron was having his helluvatime on the dance floor, a traitorous silver screw was working its way loose in the knee-joint of the prosthesis. A quarter turn, a half, another quarter, an eighth. One more twist and it was out of the threads. The knee buckled with a crack that had all of the grotesque sound of a bone snapping. And Aaron went down. In less than a second that great natural high he'd been riding for the past day—and for most of the past month—evapo-

rated into sweaty, red-faced shame. The disco music
pounded mindlessly on, but nobody was dancing now.

Half the dancers simply stared, open-mouthed, at
the figure on the floor. The other half did their best not
to look, to give the guy a little privacy in his embarrassment, but they couldn't help themselves from steal-
ing a corner-of-the-eye glance. James D. Carver Jr.
watched it all, including Aaron's struggle to get back
on his feet—he accepted no help, especially Tricia's—
and his stumble for the lobby, both hands clasped
around the offending joint. Carver shook his head.
Wasn't it too bad, he said to the man with the handle-
bar moustache, an events judge, with whom he'd been
standing.

Tricia, not having any experience in such matters,
started to follow him out, calling his name softly. But
Katie headed her off at the door. "Let me handle this,"
she said.

Aaron sat in a big leather chair off in a darker corner
of the lobby, his right hand covering his face and
the left lying listlessly in his lap. His left leg was
shoved almost straight out, heel dug into the carpet,
and the prosthesis, still unrepaired, gave a hideous
twist, like some severe dislocation, to the right pantleg.

"Aaron?"

"Go away."

"Aaron, it's me, Katie."

"I know that. Go away."

She sat on the unoccupied arm of the chair and
waited. Aaron did not acknowledge her. He waited.
She waited. In and around the doorway to the disco,
about thirty feet down the lobby, Tricia and Greg
watched and waited. So did Carver.

Aaron shifted. He pushed at his right "knee"
through the pantleg. He slapped it, not hard, a couple
of times. God, how he hated it! And the doctors who
cut his real leg off and gave him this . . . this . . . joke!
And that machine, and his father and . . . No, not his
father! It wasn't anybody's fault. Yes it was, it was

his fault, his own fault for being so stupid and careless and . . .

And . . . what? His capacity for self-contempt, for self-flagellation couldn't be *that* limited.

And . . . what the hell was he doing here anyway, pretending to be an athlete, pretending to be a whole man? Who was he trying to kid with this "it's-sort-of-a-combination-of-role-and-dive" horseshit?

He looked up at Katie, and all the fear and all the pain and all the frustration of the past six months converged, twisting his face into a terrifying mask.

"See!" he said. "See! My father was right! I am a goddamn freak!"

He raised his right fist and smashed it down on the leg, the goddamned stupid rotten ugly wooden leg.

"Aaron!" She was trembling.

"Damn it, Katie." Again the fist crashed down.

"Aaron! Stop it!"

"Look at them, Katie." He waved his arm toward the gathering crowd outside the ballroom door. "Look at them all looking at me. I saw her face, Katie, I saw her face. I saw everybody's faces . . ."

"You better get used to that, Aaron," Katie said softly, resisting the temptation to touch him, to pull his head to her breast and stroke his hair and console him. They'd come this far without sympathy entering into it and if she let that happen now, everything would have been for nothing. She would not feel sorry for Aaron, dammit! And Aaron wouldn't feel sorry for Aaron either, not if she could prevent it.

"Did you see the expression on her face?" At that very moment Aaron wanted nothing more than to be held and hidden. Katie caught Tricia coming toward them, and with a small, impatient flick of her hand—a movement Aaron could not see—waved her back. "Not yet," Katie's lips said silently. Tricia, despite her conflicts, stopped, nodded and gingerly backed off.

"Aaron," Katie said, dropping to one knee on the floor in front of him so that she could look up into his face, force him to see her, even if he didn't want to, "do you remember when we were in grade eight, do you remember Danny Horhota?"

Aaron did not appear to remember, but he did. Danny had not been one of his close friends, but he'd liked him well enough—not that it mattered anyway, considering what had happened to Danny. One winter morning Danny had been priming the old wood stove in his parents' kitchen. The wood was wet and the kitchen was icy cold. He splashed a little naptha gas on the wood. It burned, but the wood didn't and so he splashed a little more with the same result. Then he splashed a lot more and tossed in a match.

When Danny had finally returned to school the next fall, one side of his face and upper body was horribly scarred. An eye was missing and so was most of the use of his right arm. The grafts were livid and unnatural and ugly. He wore a cheap wig that only partly covered the hole where his right ear had been.

"Do you remember how we looked at him, Aaron, how we couldn't take our eyes off him, how we were too afraid to talk to him?"

Aaron nodded. He looked into Katie's eyes. Tears were running down his face, and his sobs were now audible. "I remember," he said quietly.

"And do you also remember how, after a couple of weeks, we stopped being that way. I mean we didn't sit around and talk about it, we just stopped doing it. We just started accepting and after a while we were seeing Danny Horhota again, not some scarface. It's the same, Aaron. Those people in there, from now on, will just be seeing Aaron Kornylo and not Kornylo-the-cripple. You've got to give them a chance."

Aaron brushed at his eyes with the back of his hand. He pulled up his pantleg, located the loose screw, took a dime from his pocket and effected the repairs. If people were watching, well, maybe it would be instructional for them. He slid the pantleg back down, sat up straight in the chair, and spoke directly, matter of factly, to Katie. "You know—I've got to tell you this—I'm really scared as hell about tomorrow."

"You and everybody else, Aaron, you and everybody else." She motioned Tricia to join them, and when the younger girl arrived, Katie took her hand and put it in Aaron's.

"I don't know whether or not you want to reclaim this wreck," Katie smiled, "but if you do, here he is. I'll see you—both of you—back inside later."

Tricia glanced around nervously, as if looking for guidance. But finding none, she tentatively sat on the chair arm Katie had just vacated. Aaron still hadn't really looked at her.

Aaron looked down at her hand, studied it for a moment, then lifted it to his lips and kissed it lightly. No, he was not sure why; it just felt like a good thing to do.

"Hey," she said softly, "did I ever tell you about the time I dived into the swimming pool and my top came off and I couldn't find it and I was swimming around everybody's feet and . . ."

He put his hand to her mouth.

"Listen," he said, "if you're trying to cheer me up . . ." The pause was intentional.

Tricia's face fell. She started to move away.

". . . you're succeeding." He kissed her hand again.

16

Katie could not quite fathom the look on Greg's face. It wasn't jealousy or anger, but it wasn't pleasant either. If she'd known him better—as well, say, as she knew Aaron—she could have read it from across the room. He opened his mouth to speak, thought better of it, and instead led Katie away from the doorway.

"I just heard something," he faltered, "I mean I just heard something you should probably know about. It's Carver. I just heard him saying something about Aaron . . . about Aaron's not competing . . ."

"Tomorrow? You mean tomorrow?"

"I'm not sure . . . Yes, I am sure: that's what I heard, that's what I heard him saying to one of those officials over there, the one with the moustache."

"Bastards! Bastards!" Now it was Katie who was crying.

The cab driver slowed to a crawl, squinting for house numbers. "It's one of these, Mr. Kornylo, just a little past the mayor's house. Well, he's not the mayor any more, he's a Member of Parliament now. Great guy. I took him home a couple of times."

Myles fingered the envelopes and scraps of folded paper in his inside jacket pocket and said nothing.

"There it is, Mr. Kornylo, the one with the Olds in the driveway. You want me to wait again?"

"Please," Myles said, not even looking at the meter

129

this time. He walked, like an older, wearier man, up to the white door with the brass knocker.

"Yes, can I help you?" The woman had a wary, worried look on her face. When doorbells rang after 10 P.M. in North Toronto, it usually meant trouble.

"I'd like to see Mr. Wallace, please. My name is Kornylo."

"Kornylo? Kornylo? Oh," her face relaxed, "are you related to the high jumper? Aaron?"

"Yes, ma'm. I'm his father."

Katie stayed in the john for fifteen minutes. It took her that long to finish her cry and to repair, as much as possible, the puffy damage it did her face. She re-applied her makeup, which consisted of nothing more than lipstick and a little eye shadow, and, looking straight ahead, marched back into the disco. Greg was sitting with Aaron and Tricia, looking very uncomfortable and very down. Aaron's revived spirits could not inspire him, not with him knowing what he knew. He felt like a traitor, somehow, a conspirator; and even knowing it wasn't true did not stop him from feeling that way. Tricia, on the other hand, was listening with rapt attention as Aaron described his canoe trip down the rapids. He made it into a great adventure, not quite willing to admit to relative strangers that there was any more to it than that.

Greg watched Katie all the way as she crossed the floor to their table. She shouldn't have to tell him, Greg thought, I should have done it. Well, somebody should have done it, anyway, Carver or one of those other jerks. They traded guilty glances. Katie cleared her throat. "Aaron," she forced a little smile, "do you want to dance."

"Gave it up for Lent," he replied, not sensing her tension.

"Coach's orders," she said, reaching for his hand.

John Wallace had just turned on the eleven o'clock news and was settling into his chair when, behind him, a door was opened and a male throat was cleared. He stood and half turned, and in the grey glow of the light from the TV screen he saw the face of Myles Kornylo.

"Mr. Wallace."

"Mr. Kornylo?"

"I have something important to talk about with you."

"But Mr. Kornylo, it's late. And we . . . we've been all over this matter. We can talk, if you want to, but I can tell you right now it won't do any good. Please . . . sit down. Can I offer you a drink?"

Greg's first inclination was to get up and follow Aaron and Katie out onto the dance floor, to be with her—to be with both of them—when she gave Aaron the news. In fact, he was already out of his chair, without realizing it, when he remembered that Tricia was there.

He saw her eyes following Aaron's back, and he was pretty certain he could read what was in those eyes. Funny, he thought, how just a few hours before she'd been a stranger, to him, to Aaron, to all of them. But now she was a part of them, their unofficial group, their gang, whatever it was they were.

He glanced toward the dance floor. Aaron and Katie were standing face to face. Her lips were moving, but Greg could see from the expression on Aaron's face that she hadn't dropped the bomb yet.

"Tricia," Greg swallowed, "there's something happening I think you should know about. It seems . . ."

But Tricia had been watching too, and suddenly she was out of her chair, coming around the table, fear and confusion in her eyes. Greg stepped in front of her, and caught her arm. Then he turned to see what she had seen.

Aaron's arms were flailing wildly; his face was crimson; his mouth was twisted into a snarl. Over the music, and over the forty-odd feet that separated them, Greg and Tricia heard, "Well that's just great, isn't it.

That's just bloody great" They saw him pivot on his left heel and stride toward the doorway, still crimson, still shouting, still waving his arms.

"Greg!"

"No, Tricia!" He sat her down and half-held her there. Then he looked over his shoulder at Katie, still standing where she had been, her fists clenched against her sides, tears running down her cheeks. He started across the room to her, then stopped. No. His reason overcame his instinct; Katie had to play this out by herself. She and Aaron. "Tricia," he said, turning back to her, "I think you deserve an explanation."

Wallace stood at the French doors, pretending to look out into the night, but really watching the reflection of Myles Kornylo, sitting across the room behind him. Then he turned, put his hands on the back of the rich, brown leather couch, and tried again.

"Mr. Kornylo, please be reasonable. Please try to see it our way. I mean, I feel badly about this. I'm sure the whole committee does. We want to give your son every opportunity, every chance. We're not against Aaron, we're honestly not. I mean, we all think it's marvellous what he's done. It's just . . . it's just like we told you this afternoon, about how his handicap would distract the other athletes, and . . ."

Myles checked his watch. Twenty minutes of arguing had changed nothing. Wallace did not care about the other members of the committee, that they'd changed their minds. The matter was closed. Myles suspected that Wallace was afraid of Carver, no more and no less. And he was right.

"But you never *asked* the other athletes," Myles attempted another wording of the same argument. "They've all been friends for years. I know my boy, and I know that if it was somebody else, he'd be all for it."

"Mr. Kornylo, Mr. Kornylo of course he would. Aaron's a good boy. They're all good boys, and if we asked them of course they'd say yes. But their performances would suffer for it, we know that."

"We don't know anything of the kind!" Myles had not raised his voice before. It surprised him almost as much as it did Wallace, who shrank back in fear. The big man was standing up. Should he yell for help? No, that probably wasn't called for—not yet, anyway.

"Mr. Kornylo, please, let me try it one more time: our job, the committee's job, is to create optimum conditions for Canadian athletes, and sometimes we have to do things that are good for them, even if they don't like it. It's like a father and a son, Mr. Kornylo. Surely you understand that?"

Myles sat back down. "Mr. Wallace, I surely do understand that. And if I'd made Aaron do what I wanted him to do, he wouldn't have been here to cause you people all this trouble. But he wouldn't listen to me, you know that? Every night he'd go out and jump and jump and fall and jump and get up and jump some more, and I sat there getting madder and madder and thinking how crazy he was.

"Well, maybe he was crazy, but he did it—he came back and he came here to prove it. He's as good a man as he was before. A better man. A whole man. And now you're telling him he's not. Well, he is."

Myles stopped for a second or two to put more words together in his head. He didn't see it, but there was a new expression on Wallace's face.

"What I'm trying to say, Mr. Wallace, is that if Aaron had done what was good for him—what *I* thought was good for him—he'd be moping around the farm right now, wondering if he really *was* a whole man or not. A father can be wrong, Mr. Wallace, and . . ."

"And so can a committee," Wallace finished the sentence.

By the time Katie reached the lobby, Aaron was gone. Where? Outside? She checked the streets at all three exits. Nothing. The john? Maybe. His room?

She went back into the disco. Greg and Tricia were still at the table. They weren't talking or even looking at one another, just sitting. "Aaron didn't come back here, did he?"

"No," Tricia said dully.

"Took it bad, didn't he," Greg said.

"You saw it."

Greg sat, eyes down, trying to find something useful to say. He couldn't, but he felt compelled to talk anyway, and even as he was saying, "Maybe it's for the best, maybe he realizes that," he realized how trite and stupid it sounded.

"Goddammit Greg, he wanted it! We both did. We worked for it—together. We worked hard. It was impossible, what Aaron did, but he did it. And as for your maybe-it's-for-the-best crap, well take it and stick it in Carver's ear!"

He started to rise, to touch her, to apologise for saying what he hadn't meant to say, but she pushed him back into the chair. "Stay away from me, Greg. I don't want you around me right now."

She had to find Aaron.

His room didn't answer, either to the phone calls or her knock at the door. He couldn't have been in the john that long. The bar? Aaron hardly drank anything at all, the odd beer on a hot day and a glass of wine on social occasions. But tonight? Tonight he could be in that bar.

She threaded her way between the rows of red vinyl easy chairs and the circular formica-topped tables. She peered through the calculated gloom at every youngish man she interpreted to be sitting alone. She had almost completed her circle when a voice behind her said: "Katie!"

"Clare?"

"Sit down, kid, you're blocking the view."

Katie did as she was told. Without taking her astonished eyes off Clare's face she made her way around one of the chairs at Clare's table and sort of fell backwards into it.

"Clare?" She still wasn't completely sure.

"In the flesh."

"But . . . but what are you doing here?"

"George called just after you two left. We came down to see what we could do. Myles is out doing it. Does Aaron know?"

Katie nodded. "He knows. Just found out. I just told him. I was looking for him just now. In here. I better go and try to find him."

"Freeze, kid!" She giggled. "Saw that on television. You know something, Katie, I do believe I'm a little tight."

"Clare, I . . ."

Clare dropped the laughter. She reached across the table and covered Katie's hands with her own. She spoke very deliberately, letting one thought sink in before she embarked on the next.

"Katie, it's time for us to stop nursing those boys and to let them have at whatever is bothering them and whatever they've got to do about it. Myles, he's already got his motor started and Aaron's going to have to learn to crank himself up too, whenever he stalls."

Katie sat waiting for the rest.

But there wasn't any rest.

"That's it." Clare said, the laughter back in her face. "Now have a drink with me. Do you know I haven't been in a bar myself since 1953? You're sitting across the table from a liberated woman, Katie Barlow. Stick around and you might learn something. Waiter! Innkeeper!"

17

"Mr. Kornylo!"

Who was calling him? Who did he know in this . . . this dance hall?

"Hello. I'm sorry, I . . ."

"Greg. Greg Dubois. We met in Montreal."

"Oh . . . uh . . . yes, I'm sorry. Greg, have you seen my son?" Greg didn't answer. He looked around quickly, spied an empty table off in a corner, and led Myles to it. Then he told Myles, in detail, what had happened.

All Myles said in reply was: "Where's Carver? I was told he'd be here." Before Greg could point, Myles was up and brushing past him. "Never mind," he said. "I see him."

"Who was that?" Tricia asked. She had just reentered the room after her own fruitless search for Aaron.

"Aaron's father," Greg replied, his eyes on the big man's back. "Stick around. This could be something to see."

Carol and Steve joined them, followed by a number of other athletes. "That's Aaron's father, isn't it?" Carol asked. "He's going for Carver, isn't he?"

Greg nodded, and briefly explained what was going on, as he figured it, to the others. When he finished, he tossed out an idea that had been brewing for an hour or more, from the time he'd heard about the committee's decision.

"I'm not going to pressure anybody here," he said, "but in a couple of minutes I'm going to walk over there and I'm going to tell Carver what I should have told him when I found out, that if Aaron doesn't compete, then I won't." He looked from face to face. They were not very hard to read—not very hard at all. Greg felt his eyes getting wet.

"Well of course," Carver was intoning, "it's always regrettable when one country or another uses it as political propaganda, instead of letting the athletes . . ."

"Mr. Carver."

Carver turned from his audience to look into the face of Myles Kornylo.

"Mr. Kornylo?"

"I'd like to talk to you," Myles said. The voice was as tired as the eyes, but Myles was not making a suggestion. He was issuing a command. Carver knew it and so did the men around him; they began to sink back, leaving the two men to square off against one another.

The music was softer now, as the evening wore down to the 1 A.M. closing, and the two big men could speak in low voices. First, Carver reached out his hand, but if Myles noticed he didn't acknowledge. And he must have noticed because he did not start speaking until Carver's hand was back at his side, clenching and unclenching absently.

"I'm here about Aaron, Mr. Carver."

"Well, Mr. Kornylo, I don't quite know what you expect me to say. The committee agreed. The decision was made. That's really all there is."

"No, Mr. Carver, it isn't. I've just come from talking to other members of the committee. They've all changed their minds and I have letters here to prove it. I need you to change yours because, as I understand it, the thing has to be unanimous."

Carver hadn't anticipated this. He was not a man

who was accustomed to having his positions overturned, and by God, it wouldn't happen now. He didn't
know what this hayseed had told the others, if he'd
threatened them with the newspapers—no, he wouldn't
know enough to try that, surely—or what, but James
D. Carver Jr. would not be intimidated.

"Mr. Kornylo," he began imperiously, "it is of no
consequence to me what my fellow members have
done in their own time. The committee meetings ter-
minated at 7 P.M. this evening—yesterday evening, I
believe it is now—and that is official. These . . . uh . . .
letters you hold mean absolutely nothing. Now, if
you'll excuse me . . ."

"No, sir, I won't excuse you. I came two thousand miles and Aaron . . . Aaron came a lot farther
than that, and you're going to stand here and hear me
out and if that doesn't do any good, well I'll find some
other way." He realized his voice was rising, not only
rising but getting harder, flinty. While he still could, he
brought it back under control: "I'm only asking you
to think about it a little more, like I asked the others.
Just to think about it proper."

Carver tried to push by him, to shoulder Myles out
of the way.

"Don't . . . do . . . that!" The words weren't spoken.
They were dropped, like lead pellets on a pane of thin
glass. Carver froze. He looked into Myles' eyes and
he froze harder. There was a watery sensation in his
gut, a tightness in his chest. His larynx didn't seem to
want to work. He had not experienced fear in a long
time, certainly not the fear of physical violence. James
D. Carver Jr. lived in a civilized world, where people
fought their battles in the courts, not in the alleys. But
Myles Kornylo? He was an unknown quantity, from
a world Carver had seen almost exclusively from the
first-class seats of airplanes.

Myles' huge right hand was on his left bicep, not
squeezing, but imparting a certain authority that Carver
understood. His body slumped. "Very well," he managed to get out.

"What I want to know, Mr. Carver, is if you have something personal against my son?"

"Of course not, Mr. Kornylo, why I was as proud of Aaron as . . ."

"Then why won't you let him compete?"

Carver took another deep breath, and opened his mouth to repeat what he'd already said and, if necessary, to tell Myles Kornylo that if he didn't remove his hand at once he might find himself facing assault charges.

But something stopped him, a sudden sense that he and Kornylo were no longer alone. He turned his head and found himself looking into the dark, unblinking eyes of Greg Dubois.

"Yes, Mr. Carver," Greg said evenly. "We'd all like to know that."

All? Then Carver saw the other faces, and the expression they shared, an expression that said: your move, mister. He heard the murmurs of agreement that followed Dubois' statement. He recognized Steve Catlow and Carol Coates and a couple of the others, and then he stopped trying to put names to faces. There were too many of them. A dozen. Maybe more.

Myles looked too. In an instant his anger became bewilderment. In another instant his lips curled into a smile. He released Carver's arm and stepped back.

Carver glanced nervously around the room, but there was nobody coming to his assistance. All eyes were on him, but none showed anything more than curiosity. There was no support, no sympathy there. All right, he thought, summoning back as much of his old board room composure as he could, I'll handle this myself. I'll handle the farmer *and* these ungrateful kids.

"It has nothing to do with Aaron Kornylo," he said, "and I resent the implication that it does. We—the committee—were quite properly concerned about the effects that his . . . uh . . . unfortunate disability might have on you, on the way you perform and compete. It was your well-being we were concerned about. Certainly we had nothing to gain or lose by his taking part . . ."

"We talked it over," Greg said. "We want him in."

"Greg, be reasonable. I expected you to understand. I've known your father a long time, and . . ."

"We want Aaron Kornylo to compete tomorrow."

"Impossible!" Then: "Now it really is getting late and you know what time the trials begin."

Steve Catlow stepped forward and took up a position right beside Greg. "Look," he said, "I figure on winning this thing tomorrow and going to Moscow. Next to Aaron, Greg and I were the best in Canada, and I thought I was going to take Aaron someday and be the best, even when he was okay, when he had two legs. What I'm trying to say is that if I can't go against him tomorrow, even the way things are, I just won't know if I'm better than he is. That's all I've got to say."

"That about says it for all of us," Greg added.

"Now look . . ." Carver had really had about as much of this as he was going to take. He was sweating now, and James D. Carver Jr. was a man who didn't sweat, except in pursuit of physical fitness on the running track and the squash courts of his private men's club.

"No," Greg said wearily, *"You* look. It's like this: if Aaron doesn't jump tomorrow, we don't jump tomorrow."

"Or," added Carol Coates, "do anything else tomorrow. Won't the media be fascinated? I can see the headlines now: 'Committee Bars Crippled Star' and 'Athletes Boycott Olympic Tryouts.' Won't that be fun?"

Carver sagged. There really was no way out, was there? Myles handed him a blank piece of paper and a felt-tipped pen. He turned his back and stooped slightly to give Carver a writing surface. Carver hesitated, then, impatiently, he scribbled out his consent. He handed the paper back to Myles and began to stalk away.

"My pen," Myles reminded.

Carver's first notion was to throw it, but he composed himself, returned and handed it over politely, or

at least with a façade of politeness. As he passed Greg
for the second time he muttered through closed teeth:
"You've just bought yourself a lot of trouble, my
young Mr. Dubois."

"Probably," Greg smiled sweetly.

Somewhere across the room Lieutenant Columbo
was shuffling out a doorway, then stopping and rubbing
his chin and informing the late Jack Cassidy that
there was "just one more thing, sir . . ."

Aaron wasn't watching and he wasn't listening. He
hadn't listened to the end of the news, or M*A*S*H
either. He didn't know or care what channel the set
was turned to, or what was on it. He'd flicked the set
on when he'd entered the room and just left it that
way as he lay on the bed, staring at the ceiling. Lorne
Greene appeared, selling dog food. A voice-over followed, promoting CBS's next Thursday night movie
double feature. A grating little sing-song voice revealed
a ring around somebody's collar. "Those dirty
rings . . ." another voice added. Jack Cassidy was
back, his smile more forced than before. Aaron just
stared—at the ceiling, beyond the ceiling, out to where
the past still existed. He tried to think about the future,
about what he would do next year, next month, next
week, tomorrow, but it wouldn't come, it wasn't there.
He tried to tell himself that he couldn't have gone
through life with nothing more than an ability to jump,
anyway. Eventually the crossbar would start coming
down, just the way it had gone up, half-inch by half-
inch, and if he kept doing it "for fun," well, it wouldn't
really be any fun. Even with two legs, he'd have had
to stop sometime, to fill his life with grown-up things to
amuse and distract him, to give meaning. Aaron knew
all that, but tonight that knowledge didn't help, didn't
matter a damn.

Lieutenant Columbo was about to explain to Jack
Cassidy how he'd pegged him for the killer, when a
knock came at the door.

Katie, he figured.

The knock persisted. A male voice said: "Aaron?"

Dad?

Aaron was moving toward the door before he even realized he was moving at all.

"Dad!"

In the dim light of the hall, Aaron could not see his father's eyes clearly. All he could see was the down-turned mouth and the tightness around it, and, because he couldn't know that he was being had, he gasped.

"My God, dad! What is it? What's wrong? Is it mom? Is there something wrong with mom? What . . . ?"

Then he saw the smile, a glorious untempered triumphant smile, and he stopped in mid-sentence.

"Nope," Myles said, wandering into the room and looking around and giving Aaron a chance to get his lungs working again. "At least not that I know of."

"Huh?" Aaron managed, looking around for a chair close enough to fall into and finding none.

"Well," Myles continued, "when I left her down in the bar she was doing fine, and that was just a few minutes ago. She had a Miss Katie Barlow with her, and when I left them your mother was teaching Katie and the waiter and anybody else who was listening the first twelve verses of *Roll Me Over in the Clover*."

The shock was wearing off, and Aaron no longer felt the need to sit. He was even able to take his hand off the doorknob which, for all he knew, had been holding him up. But what were they doing here, his father especially? Then he understood. They knew. They knew about the committee shooting him down —how they knew he wasn't sure, but they'd found out and they'd come down to . . . what?

The memory of the night before flooded back, and he saw his father as he was then, and he heard the words again that his father had spoken, the cruel words. "Oh," he said, looking away, "you've heard. Yeah, the freak show's been cancelled." Then he stared hard into his father's face, eager, for once, to see the anger form.

But Myles' expression didn't change.

Okay, Aaron thought, we'll try it again.

"Did you hear me?" he said, his own anger escalating. "I said the freak show's canceled! Over! Finis! Kaput! What did you do, come down to gloat?"

Come on, old man!

At last Myles dropped his smile, and Aaron poised himself for what he was sure was coming. He waited, preparing the counterattack in his mind.

Come on, old man!

"Aaron," Myles said, gently and a little sadly, "Aaron, I didn't mean it the way it sounded, like I thought you were a freak or anything like that, I just . . ."

"Why not?" Aaron interrupted, half in bitterness and half in a show of self-pity. "It was true. You were right. Father knows best, right? You and Robert Young. Well, I guess the committee knows best too. I won't be out there embarrassing anybody tomorrow."

"No, you won't," Myles said, still gently. "But you'll be out there—at least if you still want to." He handed Aaron the sheaf of letters from his pocket and, while his son read them, he stepped over and flicked off the TV set, now featuring nothing but buzzing colored snow.

Aaron finished the letters. He folded them carefully and put them in his pocket. He looked toward Myles, who was not looking back. He was by the window pretending to be watching the goings-on in the street below. There were tears in his eyes too.

"Dad . . ."

"Some of your friends downstairs, Greg and some others, they were a big help. You've got good friends, Aaron, good friends."

Aaron walked to the window. It was impossible to talk. Then he did something he'd never done before, not that he could remember anyway. He reached out and touched his father's arm. Again he opened his mouth, and again no words came out.

"As for what I think, for what your mother and I both think, well I think you should go through with it tomorrow. But it's up to you, Aaron. That's how it should be."

Slowly, Myles turned around. Just as slowly and a great deal more awkwardly he put his arms around his son, and while Aaron cried softly, Myles finished what he had to say.

"When the accident happened, I was like you, I guess. I thought it was the end of everything. And even when you and Katie started showing me different, well, I still didn't understand. But you showed me different, Aaron." He stopped talking and held Aaron even more tightly. And Aaron's spinning mind tried to remember the last time he'd been in those arms. Ten years? Fifteen? Not since he was a little boy, anyway. He was surprised at how good it still felt.

"When you were born, Aaron," his father continued, "the only question I asked was did you have the right number of everything—arms, legs, fingers, toes. I guess a parent wants to make sure his child's got everything that's coming to him. Aaron, you're just as whole and complete a person right now as you were the first day your mother trusted me to hold you. What I'm trying to say is that I love you and respect you and . . . and I hope you'll forgive me for being so slow in getting around to saying it, and showing it." For a long, long moment neither moved. When Aaron's breathing became quiet again, Myles began to extricate himself.

"I think we'd better get down there and rescue that bar from your mother and Katie," he said. "Don't these big-city bartenders know enough to throw folks out when it's time to go home?"

But they only made it halfway down the hall when the elevator doors opened and spilled out two somewhat familiar females. Clare and Katie, silly grins plastered all over their faces, were now marching toward them, arm in arm, slurring the words to *The North Atlantic Squadron*.

"See what I mean," Myles stage-whispered into his son's ear.

Clare stopped short—which meant Katie did too,
"Indeed, I do," Aaron stage-whispered back.
almost falling backward in the process—and eyed the
two men up and down. "The cabin boy, the cabin boy,
the . . ." she sang, then stopped and put a finger up to
her own lips.

". . . the dirty little nipper," Katie continued. Then
she stopped too and cocked her head toward Myles
and Aaron.

"Ignore them," Clare instructed her. "They're probably sober."

"Stand aside, Aaron," Katie said, removing her arm
from Clare's. "You too, Myles." Myles? "I'm going to
bed."

As she stood outside her door, fumbling for her key,
she remembered her manners and turned to the three
of them. "Night, Clare. Night, Aaron." Then: "Night,
Myles."

Aaron, still dressed, lay on the bed, thinking about
his father and trying to sort out the events of the past
two hours. He told himself he should be happy, but it
wasn't quite there. Something nagged, something was
interfering with the seemingly settled new scheme of
things. But he couldn't find it.

After a few minutes of staring at the ceiling, he rose,
undressed and unstrapped his prosthesis. Not wanting
to lie down again just yet, and now knowing exactly
why, he hopped into the bathroom and switched on
the shower, as hot as his hand could stand it.

He let the water beat down on him for what he
guessed was about ten minutes before reaching for the
soap. Just then, he heard the phone ringing—or
thought he did. He twisted off the faucets. Yes, it was
the phone. Two o'clock in the morning. Whoever said
that the one sure way to get people to call you up was
to get into the bathtub was right. Gripping the sink for
support, Aaron vaulted out of the tub and reached the
phone in the middle of its ninth ring.

"Aaron?" the unsure-sounding voice said. "Aaron, it's me. Tricia. I'm sorry it's so late, I hope I didn't wake you . . ."

"Naah," Aaron assured her, checking his watch to see that it was closer to 2:30 than 2 A.M. "I was just in the shower."

Tricia started to apologise for that, but he stopped her.

"Say," he said, "something just occurred to me: aren't you running in the morning? Shouldn't you be asleep?"

"No," she said. "The afternoon, same as you. Couldn't sleep anyway." After a short silence, she said, "I guess you know all about what happened downstairs?"

"Most of it. My father told me. I'd love to have been there."

More silence. The second hand on his watch swept past the three, the four, the five . . .

"Aaron?" Her voice was smaller, different, more tentative. "Aaron, I . . . uh . . . hope you won't think I'm awful but . . . uh . . . would you . . . uh . . . like some company or anything? I mean, like now?"

The second hand swept past the eleven, the twelve, the one . . .

"Aaron?"

"Tricia," he said at last, "I think I want a lot of your company. In fact, you may be sorry you made the offer. But tomorrow. And after tomorrow. It's funny, you know, but I feel like I have a lot of things to work out right now. It's been a kind of weird day. Do you mind? I mean I hope you don't mind. I mean . . . you know what I mean?" He still wasn't sure why he'd said and done what he'd said and done, but he knew he didn't regret it.

"You sure have a way with words, Aaron Kornylo. What time do you want to meet for breakfast?"

The pre-dawn light was filtering through the window before Aaron at last slept, and even then his body jerked and convulsed to raspy dreams. He was in Montreal again, running in slow, slow motion toward the uprights, his legs full of pain and tension, his lungs shrunken. His body rose like a balloon, drifting, and the crossbar seemed to be drifting too, and there was no sound around him, and he could see that he was naked and all he could think of was getting over, down into the pit, burying his shame and embarrassment. He rolled over the bar and began to fall . . .

He woke, and the bed was sweat-soaked; he slept again and the dream returned, almost as before. But this time he did not wake, not until he was in the pit. He could see the crowd, his mother and his father and Greg and Katie and . . . yes, there was Carver! And Carver was laughing, though no sound came out. Then everybody was laughing, sixty thousand people were laughing, their faces distorted, their fingers all pointed at him.

And there was still no sound.

Then Carver came toward him, followed by the others, and they stood around him in a huge circle, still laughing and pointing, and he looked for his father and his mother and Katie to come, to help him, but they weren't there anymore, just Carver and all those strangers looming over him, sucking away his air . . .

He woke again. The room was brighter. In a few minutes he was breathing normally and his heartbeat was regular. Two hours sleep, maybe three at the most. But he had to get up. Couldn't take another dream like that. Besides, what if *the* dream came, the great auger chasing him, running him down, grinding his foot, his calf, his knee . . .

His eyes burned and his head pounded and there was a tightness across the small of his back where he'd arched it, God knows how many times, in the fitful hours of sleep. With great effort, he got himself into a sitting position but the bile, which had risen to sear inside his chest, did not recede; it corroded his throat now, and it was all he could do to make the bathroom before he started to gag and vomit.

For a long time he just sprawled on the cold white tiles of the bathroom floor, his back half-propped against the door, and only when he was sure the nausea had passed did he finally flush the toilet. Then, using the sink, he pulled himself upright, an act that almost totally sapped what was left of his strength. Half-hopping, half-sliding along the wall, he made it back to the bed.

18

"Aaron?" Knock-knock-knock. "Aaron?" Knock-knock. "Aaron!"

"Yes, yes!" he blinked, confused. Where was he? "Just a second." Toronto. Hotel. Sun's out. "Yeah, I'll be right there."

There was a worried look on Tricia's face. "It's nearly eleven o'clock, Aaron. I was waiting for you in the coffee shop and I started to get concerned when you weren't there. I know I was being silly, but . . . Aaron, are you sure you're all right?"

"Yeah, it's okay. Trouble getting to sleep, that's all. Happened before. Lousy dreams. What time did you say it was? Eleven o'clock?"

"Nearly. Want me to wait downstairs?"

"Yeah. Sure. Be down in a few minutes." Then: "Is Katie there?"

"She was. She and Greg went over to watch the morning stuff. She said to tell you she'd meet you there."

"Okay." He didn't hurt anymore, and the nausea seemed to have disappeared, but he was still weak and weary, and wishing, as he had countless times in his sleepless hours, that he was somewhere else.

In the privacy of the shower, he talked to himself out loud: "Okay, Kornylo, you got what you wanted, and now you're wondering if you really want it. Well, you must have or you wouldn't have gone through all that crap to get here. Come on man, snap out of it." He

149

continued the argument, adding and subtracting points on both sides, until he limped out of the room about twenty minutes later. By the time he found Tricia in the coffee shop he had regained some part of both his lost strength and lost confidence.

"No food," he told the waitress. "Large orange juice, large milk, coffee."

Tricia wore her worried look again.

"It's okay," Aaron reassured her, "I never eat before I jump."

"Greg," Katie said, touching his thigh as they sat in the stands half-watching men's javelin, "could you check out the dressing room again? It's after noon and there's still no sign of him."

Greg patted her leg and rose, walked a few steps down and neatly vaulted the rail. He stopped to wave before heading off once more to the dressing room. But his journey was cut short, because as he reached the mouth of the tunnel, Aaron was emerging, his prosthesis—but not his limp—hidden in the slightly-gaudy Olympic team sweatsuit. "Hi man," Greg said. "You okay? Katie was worried."

"Just overslept," Aaron said, clapping Greg on the shoulder and leading him back from whence he had come. The smile was still a bit forced, but it was beginning to feel more natural. "I want to thank you for what you did last night. It couldn't have been easy."

Greg shrugged self-consciously.

"No," Aaron persisted, "I mean it."

"Well," Greg said, nodding toward where Katie was sitting, "my motives may not have been all that pure, you know. Besides, it wasn't just me, it was everybody. I think old Steve might have actually swung it."

Katie had joined them on the field by now so Aaron decided to let the subject drop. He would thank everybody individually before the day was over.

"You okay?" Katie asked. She was looking at him with her head cocked to one side, studying him, and when he gave her the oversleeping story he could see she wasn't totally buying. When they were alone, coach and competitor, she asked: "You had the dream again, didn't you."

"No," he replied, "not *the* dream. But others. I didn't sleep very well. A lot of things on my mind. Kind of natural, I suppose, considering."

"Pain?"

"A few twinges at breakfast and on the way over in the taxi. Nothing special, nothing I can't handle. It'll feel better when I've got the prosthesis off—which I might as well do right now. Have you got the crutches?"

Myles paced the hotel lobby, checking his watch, checking the elevator doors, checking the watch again. Where the hell was that woman? Twenty-two minutes ago he'd left her behind the closed bathroom door, brushing her teeth for at least the fourth time and moaning little moans. Her garbled voice had promised five minutes, and if he couldn't wait five bloody minutes he could go on without her and she'd meet him there.

In fact, Myles started to do just that, but by the time he reached the main doors of the hotel his irritation had worn off, and he was reminding himself he really was in one hell of a good mood.

He felt a light touch on his arm and found himself looking down into one of the great forlorn faces of all time.

"Clare!"

"Stop shouting, Myles. I hate it when you shout." She reached up to touch her temple, winced, and brought the hand down to her side, where it just sort of dangled.

And her eyes! Myles tried not to look.

"I can't go out there, Myles," she said, waving a hand weakly toward the door and the bright, sunlit street beyond. "I just opened the drapes to see what kind of day it was. My head nearly exploded."

He led her—literally—into the hotel's drug store and stood her before the sunglasses rack.

"Try these," he suggested.

Gingerly Clare put on the sunglasses and looked out the drugstore window into the noonday street. "No," she winced, "darker."

"Shouldn't have drunk so much," Myles teased.

"Thanks," she muttered back, "I really needed to hear that. Is it time yet?"

He consulted the watch. They had about half an hour and he told her so.

"I wonder," Clare said, touching her stomach lightly, "if this drugstore sells bicarbonate of soda?"

Tricia finished her warm-ups and joined Aaron and Katie briefly while she waited for the women's hundred meters to be announced. Aaron was doing one-handed, one-legged push-ups, and Katie was standing just to one side, counseling. "Remember: take your time when you get there, there's no rush, nobody's rushing you."

Aaron grunted. "How many is that?" he managed to get out without breaking his rhythm.

"Forty-eight, forty-nine, fifty," she read from the small counter in her hand. "Take five."

"Hi," Tricia said. "Feeling better?"

The question was not lost on Katie. What she took it to mean was that Aaron had been feeling worse than he'd admitted, and maybe still was. But before she could start grilling him—both of them—Tricia was asking: "Katie, it just occurred to me—aren't you in these trials too?"

"Vancouver. In two weeks. They split them up for some reason, to try to generate more national interest I guess. Why were you asking Aaron if he was feeling better?"

"Katie," Aaron interrupted, "I told you I had a bad night and that's all it was and I'm better now. So if you'll hold my feet—my foot—I'd like to do a few sit-ups."

Again Katie's pursuit of the truth was stymied, this time by the crackling, echoing voice of the public address announcer. *"Women's hundred meters about to begin, northwest corner of the stadium . . ."*

"A kiss for luck?" Tricia asked.

"A kiss for luck," Aaron confirmed. "But you'll have to come down here."

"There's Aaron," Myles indicated. "And Katie."

"But who's that blonde girl kissing Aaron?" Clare asked, brushing a candy wrapper off the wooden seat before dropping into it heavily.

"Don't know. She was with Greg and the others last night. Wait, somebody introduced us. It's Tricia something-or-other."

They sat in silence, waiting for Aaron or Katie to see them and wave.

"Myles," Clare said, "I know this doesn't sound like me at all. Maybe it's all the rush, or the hangover or I don't-know-what, but ... but I'm scared for him. I keep wondering, what if he doesn't make it?"

Myles put his big hand over his wife's small one. "Even if he doesn't make it," he said, "he'll make it."

"Yes," she said. "Of course he will."

Tricia took an early lead and held it for the first seventy-five meters. Then, kicking hard toward the finish line, something popped in her left calf. She limped in fourth of seven, out of contention. She sat on the soft grass, kneading at the calf, tears of frustration and pain running down her cheeks. The doctor arrived before Aaron and Katie, and was probing with his practised fingers when they finally got there.

"Oh, Aaron," Tricia sobbed, oblivious to the ministrations of the physician and to the presence of three of the other sprinters who had gathered around her, "I blew it. I had it and I blew it!"

"Never mind that," Aaron said sternly. "Are you all right?"

"She's fine," the doctor said, looking up and, seeing a one-legged athlete towering over him, doing a double take. "It's a pulled muscle, that's all. Tough loss, but there'll be other days ... You're Aaron Kornylo, aren't you?"

Aaron nodded.

"You going to jump?"

Aaron nodded again.

"You are one hell of a guy," the doctor said.

As Aaron dropped down beside Tricia the others, including the doctor, began to move away.

"Oh, Aaron, I was so close," Tricia said, rubbing at her eyes with her hands. He gave her his towel and she used that instead. "I saw the tape, and I could hear the girl coming up on the right and I kicked, I guess I kicked too hard. So much for Moscow."

"Tricia, it's not the end of the world, you know. Moscow isn't everything." He heard what he said and it stunned him. Moscow *was* everything. Moscow was why he was here. "There's always L.A., I mean, and lots of track meets in between."

There was nothing more he could think of to say. He kiss her forehead lightly, then rose. Tricia, unsteadily, followed suit. "Can you walk?" Aaron asked.

"I think so." Yes, she could put weight on the leg.

"I'd lend you my crutches, but I'm going to need them for the next little while. A kiss for luck?"

"A kiss for luck."

"There's your mom and dad," Katie waved into the third row of stands, just behind their bench. Aaron located them, smiled and tipped his imaginery hat. They waved back, but his mother's was perceptibly less enthusiastic than his father's.

"Katie," Aaron said out of the side of his mouth, "what in the hell did you do to my mother last night. Sunglasses. She's never worn sunglasses in her life. And look at her . . ."

"All I did was help her remember a glorious night she had back in 1953, that's all. Besides, you saw her. Don't you think it was worth it?"

Aaron shrugged. Of course he did.

"Aaron . . ."

"Yeah."

"Remember now, when you go, let the power come off your toes. It starts in the thigh and goes all the way down to the toes. You got that?"

"Yeah."

"Sure you're all right?"

Not entirely, but it would pass. Just a throb in the stump, that was all.

"Lots better than you, that's for sure."

"What?"

"I just noticed that you're a touch green around the gills too. And your breathing needs a little work. That must have been one hell of a night, back there in 1953. Want an aspirin?"

"I've taken some, thanks. Now let's go over it . . ."

"*Men's high jump,*" the PA boomed. "*Center field.*"

"Ah," Aaron said, "the moment of truth." He wasn't smiling when he said it.

The bar was at six-nine and Steve Catlow, the first man up in the alphabetically ordered schedule, took it with ease. In fact, he hadn't even bothered to take off his sweatsuit. The applause might have been louder except that he was out of the pit and ambling back to the bench before half the people realized the event was actually underway. Aaron clapped politely and waved, but Steve didn't notice. He just sat a few feet away and gazed intently into space.

"*Next contestant, men's high jump, at six feet, nine inches, Number 37, Greg Dubois.*" The crowd, especially Myles Kornylo, applauded.

"Hey, Greg." It was Aaron.

Greg looked over his shoulder as he jogged to his starting position. "Yeah?"

"Do it, man."

Greg answered with a wave.

As they watched, Katie, completely unconsciously, gripped Aaron's leg. "Now don't tense up," she was saying almost mechanically. "Got to stay loose."

"Katie . . ."

"You can make this height, no problem."

"Katie!"

"Yes? Yes? What?"

"You're putting my leg to sleep."

"Oh. Sorry."

Like Steve Catlow, Greg took the jump without trouble, leaving a couple of inches of daylight between himself and the crossbar.

"Next contestant, men's high jump at six feet, nine inches, Number 65, Aaron Kornylo."

Light applause. Then, as Aaron stood and fitted the crutches under his armpits, near-silence. Then silence itself, a hush. And then, suddenly, the whole stadium erupted. Athletes, former athletes, judges, friends, relatives and people who'd just wandered in were on their feet. Crimson-faced and sweating into the pads of his crutches. Aaron waited till it subsided.

He fused his mind and body. He let the crutches drop. He swung his arms, making the correction for balance. He began his approach. There were perhaps four thousand people in Varsity Stadium that afternoon, and at that very moment, not one was breathing in *or* out.

Down, down. Down into the toes.

Now!

Up! Higher! Higher!

He landed clearly, looking up. The crossbar might as well have been welded to the uprights. His arms raised themselves. His fists made themselves. He must have shouted something because his mouth was wide open, but his words were lost forever in the great surging noise of the crowd, a tumult that followed him all the way back to the bench, and for another two minutes or so thereafter.

"They want you to stand," Katie said, prodding at his ribs.

He did, and waved. The crowd responded anew— and, if it were possible, louder. Finally, it stopped and sat. Charlie Thomas, the Mohawk kid from eastern Ontario, also cleared the bar, but the two other contestants, who were still in their mid-teens, failed on both attempts. There was now a field of four.

"What's the matter, Aaron?"

"Nothing."

Greg wandered over and plunked himself down beside Steve. "You wanted to know how he does it? Well, that's how he does it."

"It's a real mother, isn't it," Steve said, standing and, for the first time, peeling off his sweatsuit, "a real mother. But I'm still going to take him."

Clare tugged at her husband's arm. "Myles" she whispered, "there's something the matter with Aaron."

"Come on, Clare, there's nothing wrong." There *was*, of course, and he could sense it as well as she could, but he wasn't going to admit it, he wasn't going to tell her that.

If Steve Catlow was thrown off by Aaron's first jump, he didn't show it. If anything, his six-ten effort was more businesslike than his first. He knew—and he was letting the whole stadium know—that anything under seven feet had become, for him, nothing much more than a warm-up. In fact, he no longer even trained under that height and he was making it three out of four times with consistency.

"He's looking awful good, isn't he?" Aaron nudged Katie. "Been doing a little wood-sheddin' since Montreal."

"Forget it," she said, watching Catlow lope back to the bench. "You're not going against him, you're going against the crossbar. Remember that: you're only going against the crossbar."

"Yeah." The pain in the stump was one stop below the blinding stage and threatening to escalate. Aaron forced himself not to rub the area, to telegraph what was happening there and along the neural passageways to his brain. But when he spoke his words came through tightly clamped teeth; his breathing was rapid and shallow; and he had to shake his head every few seconds to disperse the pulsating red mists that ran across his field of vision.

"Aaron, please tell me . . ."

"It'll pass," he said. "Come on, Greg!"

Greg probably deserved more than the polite applause he got, but he and everybody in competition knew that the crowd was saving up its emotions for the incredible one-legged kid from Saskatchewan.

"Your turn," he said as he returned to the bench. "The Force be with you."

Except for the muffled traffic in the street beyond, there was no sound. Even the athletes stopped whatever they happened to be doing and drifted as close to the high-jump area as they were permitted. Whispered asides, what few of them there were, were not acknowledged.

Aaron swayed.

Katie opened her mouth to shout, then closed it.

Clare looked away.

Myles narrowed his eyes.

The crowd took another breath and held it.

Aaron forced all of his remaining power into the left leg. He started his approach. No pain, no pain! When he landed in the pit he screamed, but nobody heard it, lost as it was in the roar of the crowd. The crossbar stayed right where it was.

When his eyes refocused, Katie and Greg were standing over him, reaching for him, hauling him up. "Just the crutches," he managed. "Just hand me the crutches."

The young doctor who'd treated Tricia's leg met them halfway back to the bench. "Phantom limb, isn't it?" he asked.

"Yeah," Aaron grunted. "It'll stop. Always stops."

"I can give you something—but I'm afraid that you'll have to call it a day . . ."

"Nothing. Not a day. Be okay." Then he remembered. "Thanks," he said.

"Aaron," Katie said as they were alone once more on their corner of the bench, "I think we should stop it. Now, I mean."

"No way. One more. One more."

When Myles saw the young man with the familiar black bag standing over his son, he couldn't pretend— to Clare or himself—any longer. He reached for her hand.

"There *is* something wrong," he admitted.

"Yes," Clare said, taking his hand in both of hers and fighting back the thickening in her throat.

Charlie Thomas failed at six-ten. He tried again and failed again.

The pain wasn't getting any better, but at least it wasn't getting any worse, except for the spasms which, when they came, almost rendered Aaron unconscious. But at least they were blessedly short-lived. He rubbed at the stump now, for the whole world to see. Couldn't hide it any more.

He didn't see Steve Catlow make six-eleven on his first try, or Greg Dubois miss on his. His eyes were shut against the latest, worst and most enduring rush of torment.

He heard a jumble of words from far, far away that ended with his name.

"Tell them no," Aaron said.

"But you'll have to withdraw," Katie said. "I'll . . ."

"No. Not withdraw. Pass. For seven feet."

"You sure?"

Aaron turned his head slowly and looked at her. She rose, collared the closest event official with a walkie-talkie and gave him her instructions.

"Something's happening down there now," Myles said, starting to climb out of his seat.

Clare pulled him gently back. Her instinct—or was it nothing more than twenty-three years of watching and understanding her son?—told her that somehow, everything was going to work out. "It's okay, he's just passing so he can save himself for a higher jump. It's in the rules."

"Now how in hell do you know that?"

"I know a lot of things, Myles Kornylo, a lot of things you don't know. Now sit down, you're making my poor head spin."

In a few seconds the public address announcer, taking liberties, confirmed what Clare had just said. *"Ladies and gentlemen,"* the crackling, metallic voice intoned,

"we have some good news and some bad news ..."
The voice let its little departure-from-form settle in.
*"The bad news is that Aaron Kornylo is passing on his
first attempt at six feet, eleven inches."* When the groans
subsided, the voice resumed its explanation: *"The good
news is that he remains in contention. The rules allow
all jumpers to waive a lower height and go on to a
higher one instead."* The voice clicked off and its
ears listened to the applause below.

Greg's leg grazed the bar, and all the way down he
watched in helpless fascination as it bounced, in ever-
so-slow motion, on its brackets, then settled contented-
ly in place.

Aaron raised two fingers to the nearby official, indicating he was passing his second six-eleven try—a
formality, but a necessary one. The pain seemed to be
ebbing. Or was that just wishful thinking. No, it *was* better; the red fog was lifting; the arched, bunched muscles
were beginning to relax. The seconds passed more
quickly now, and with each one Aaron's sense of well-
being increased. He actually thought of a joke, that old
joke about the guy who is beating himself on the head
with a hammer, and his friend says, "Doesn't that hurt?"
and the guy says, "Yeah, but it feels so good when I
stop."

But he waited. To be sure.

*"Men's high jump. First attempt. Seven feet. Steve
Catlow."*

The crossbar was unmolested.

*"Men's high jump. First attempt. Seven feet. Greg
Dubois."*

"A one-legged high jumper in the Olympics," the
voice beside Katie Barlow said, shocking her attention
away from Greg's slow walk to the starting position.

"What?"

"Ridiculous," Aaron said. She'd been right: there was
laughter in the voice, and there was laughter on the
face. Was he going nuts?

"But . . . but, you're serious!"

"Yep."

"But Aaron, if you make this, you're in. You're going to Moscow. It's what you wanted . . ."

"I don't want the Olympics." His voice contained neither humor nor anger nor any other emotion. "I don't think now I ever wanted it."

"Well what in the hell are you doing here?"

"Tell you in a sec," he said. "Let's watch Greg now."

When Greg's back hit the mats, Aaron was standing and cheering before Katie was. Her puzzled face reflecting her puzzled mind, she couldn't even manage a smile for the man she loved as he strode back to the bench.

"Men's high jump. First attempt. Seven feet. Aaron Kornylo."

"Well, what the hell . . ." Katie was suddenly aware of the silence, and the volume and the anger of her own voice. "What the hell are we doing here?" she said in a whisper.

"Proving something. And we have."

"And you don't want to see how far you can go?"

He took her face in his hands and held it, feeling her cheeks grow hot, seeing the flush and the confusion in her eyes. "Katie," he said softly, so that only she could hear, "remember how the other night you said the most important thing for you was for me to understand you?"

Her eyes answered yes.

"Well, I'm only asking the same from you." He kissed her forehead and stood back. "And Katie . . ."

She looked up. "Yes, Aaron?"

"I *know* how far I can go."

Aaron turned and swung himself across the twenty or so feet to the starting position.

"Ladies and gentlemen . . ." But the metallic voice was lost, lost forever in the roaring crescendo, in more sound than four thousand voices had ever made before.

Aaron stood, head down. It was Montreal again, it . . .

No it wasn't.

He stepped backward one step, turned and looked at

Katie, standing where he'd left her, looking all-and-very-much-alone.

"Katie," he shouted. Then, realizing that the crowd had gone suddenly silent, he dropped down to a normal speaking voice. "Katie," he said, letting each word come out distinctly, one at a time, "this one is just for you."

When she finally realized, when she finally smiled, he turned and dropped the crutches.

The world began to drop away, all sights, all colors, all sounds. All that remained was him. Him and the crossbar. Nothing above it, nothing below it, nothing on either side, just a length of laminated, varnished hardwood, hanging up there in space, seven feet above the ground.

Aaron swung his arms, getting the balance, getting the rhythm. The power was charging through him. Too much? No. Pouring into the leg now, staying there, doubling, tripling.

He began his approach, looking straight ahead now, into the blur. No need to look for the bar, he knew where it was, his body knew where it was. Two more hops. One more. Bend the knee. All power in the toes now.

Up now. Dive now. Tuck now. Falling.

He lay there in the soft vinyl-covered foam rubber, not moving, not breathing, not even opening his eyes, listening for the explosion of sound. One heartbeat. Two . . .

Something landed on top of him, knocking out his breath. Not something. Somebody. Katie! She was kissing him, hugging him, pounding on his chest, screaming something he couldn't hear because the four thousand voices were now forty thousand; no, four hundred thousand.

Somebody was grabbing his hand, pumping it. Greg! And behind him Steve Catlow was jumping up and down, motioning more people over, pointing down at Aaron. And there was Tricia, pushing her way through the gathering crowd, reaching for his other hand.

Katie bounced away and Aaron saw his mother, just standing there quietly. Their eyes met and held for a half-second and then, of all things, she winked. Aaron winked back. Then he let his eyes wander past her, along the tanned, muscular arm that was on her shoulder, up the sinewy neck, to the closed, trembling smiling mouth, to the warm blue eyes that laughed and blinked away tears.

Aaron closed his eyes and lay back again, letting all the joy he'd ever felt pour out to these wonderful, crazy people. Then he remembered something—one last thing—he'd forgotten to do.

He looked up at the crossbar, and he raised his clenched fists, to it and to the sky. And then he began to laugh.

ABOUT THE AUTHOR

JOHN GAULT was born in Cornwall, Ontario, in 1941. After attending the University of Toronto, he wrote for most of the major Canadian newspapers and magazines. For three years he was first a senior editor then executive editor at *MacLeans*. His book, *The Fans Go Wild*, was published by new Press; his novel, *Nightbreak*, which will be published by Bantam Books, has been acquired for the films.

THE MANAWAKA SERIES

by

Margaret Laurence,
*Canada's most celebrated novelist,
Winner of the Governor-General's
Award*

The Manawaka stories, set in the most
famous fictional town in Canada, offer a
clear-eyed vision of Canadian land and
people.

This skilled story teller balances humor and
pathos as she portrays the human condition through characters struggling to come
to terms with themselves and with the
world.

**THE STONE ANGEL
A JEST OF GOD
THE FIRE-DWELLERS
A BIRD IN THE HOUSE
THE DIVINERS**

Seal Books

Available in paperback at all good bookstores
across Canada.   MSML-1

SEAL BOOKS

Offers you a list of outstanding fiction, non-fiction and classics of Canadian literature in paperback by Canadian authors, available at all good bookstores throughout Canada.

The Mark of Canadian Bestsellers

The #1 Canadian bestseller
by Charles Templeton

ACT OF GOD

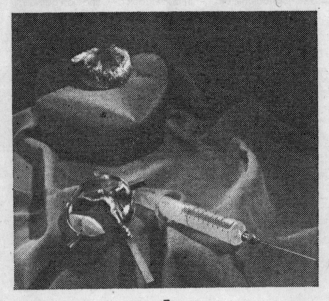

"Superb! I was spellbound!" —Arthur Hailey

"An absolute winner!" —William Stevenson

This year's most controversial novel! Read the blockbuster bestseller about a secret so momentous it threatens to change the course of history.

A Seal Book/On Sale Everywhere

Pierre Berton's
#1 Canadian bestseller
is now a Seal paperback

THE DIONNE YEARS

A THIRTIES MELODRAMA

The birth of the Dionne quintuplets to a poor Ontario farm wife in 1934 was a miracle. Their story is the story of Canada in the '30s, when beer was a nickel, swing was king, and five baby girls symbolized the hopes and dreams of an era.

 A Seal Book
On Sale Everywhere